Lainey Lainey

Lainey Lainey

Lisa Tenzin-Dolma

Published by Phoenix Rising Press 2018

© Copyright Lisa Tenzin-Dolma 2018

LAINEY LAINEY

ISBN 978-1-5272-2354-7

Book formatted by www.bookformatting.co.uk.
Cover Design by Subtifuge Designs

Contents

For my friend Lainey, who let me borrow her name

CHAPTER 1

LAINEY

I'd better start with a confession. I, Lainey Morgan, at the age of 16 years and 1 month (so should know better), am now officially a Love Rat. I have joined the ranks of the people I most despise.

There, I've said it. Or rather, written it. Before you ask - yes, I'm deeply mortified and ashamed of myself and I promise I won't do it again. Admitting it makes me feel even worse, and I'm pretty sure that everything that happened afterwards was the universe's way of punishing me.

I blame the rain. There's something about precipitation that has a weird effect on me. Sometimes I want to dance through it, stretching out my arms to the heavens, but that wet weekend I was in the mood for snuggling under a blanket on the sofa, watching reruns on TV. However, when you have Full Responsibility for a dog (in my case, Molly the young wolfhound-greyhound mix), you have no choice but to put on your wellies and raincoat and slosh through Victoria Park for the afternoon round of exercise, getting wetter and muddier by the second.

If I'd ignored Molly's pleading brown eyes and softly wagging tail, or had just taken her for a short walk instead of following her favourite route, it wouldn't have happened. I wouldn't have seen Kieran Kamau, ex-boyfriend, ex-BOMD (Boy of My Dreams) and Love Rat, in a heap beside the carved tree trunk, crying even harder than the rain.

Now, to those of you who've been living on Planet Zod and don't know who Kieran is, he's the boy everyone, but everyone, wants to get close to since his band, Dark Matter, won on Teen Star last year. That's why he became a Love Rat, because I'm no competition for girls like supermodel Dahlia Dean, who was the reason for Kieran's lapse of interest. I have far too many BHDs (Bad Hair Days). Not that the delectable Ms. Dean landed Kieran for long. A few more broken hearts have been strewn along the wayside since then.

Kieran and I didn't see each other at all for a while, and we don't see each other very often nowadays, but at least we're friends again. My heart is mended (or I thought it was) and the past is the past, as my Mum says – and the less I think about the past year with her, the better. I mean, not many mums uproot their daughters just as love strikes for the first time (with Kieran), whisk them away to the Commune From Hell in deepest Nottinghamshire (Ivy House – I strongly urge you to avoid that place of never-ending misery), then finally relent and return to civilisation with a new man in tow.

Well, what would you do if you found your ex-BOMD hunched over, soaking wet and covered in mud and leaves, sobbing his heart out? I hung back, trying to shush Molly, who strained at the lead and whined in her desperation to run over and say hello. She really likes Kieran, but then Molly likes everyone. She's an expert at unconditional love. I try hard to emulate her, but there are certain people who make me so mad when I even think of them that I know I'll never succeed.

I started to walk backwards, knowing that Kieran may not appreciate being seen looking less than his usual cool self. Molly turned as if she was about to come quietly, then leaped in the air and with a Herculean effort whipped the lead out of my hand and galloped at top speed to plonk herself on what she could find of Kieran's lap, giving him a vigorous face-wash as she landed. Kieran gave a yell of shock and then recognised his assailant and put his arms around her. Fortunately, Molly is one of those dogs who actively invites hugs, unlike our neighbour's Jack Russell, Fred the Destroyer, who takes a chunk out of anyone foolish enough to attempt any demonstration of affection.

Kieran looked up, eyes red, tears mingling with the rain, and his beautiful spirally curls all sodden and elongated. I stood awkwardly a short distance away and gave an embarrassed half-wave. He returned it from somewhere around Molly's back, looking equally mortified. I couldn't help thinking that at least it was only me who'd seen him. The Paparazzi would have hurled themselves into an orgiastic feeding frenzy and shed their own blood to get pictures of this on the cover of *Tween Dreaming Magazine*.

"Sorry we disturbed you," I said, moving closer and trying vainly to extricate Molly, who now had her paws on Kieran's shoulders and was clinging on as if she thought this would put the pieces back together again. Kieran grunted something into Molly's soaking wet fur.

As it was impossible to get any wetter, I sat down beside him and held the nearest hand. No point in asking him whether he was okay. Poor Kieran lost his Mum, Estelle, to the Evil Cancer last year. It was Estelle who made sure that Kieran and I became friends again just before she died. She was like a surrogate mum to me, I missed her a lot, and I just couldn't imagine how hard it must have been for Kieran to go out and do gigs and be photographed all the time straight afterwards. His record company said he had to Fulfil His Commitments and he had a small role in a film to do, too.

We sat there in silence (well, Molly was huffing and puffing a bit, trying to find bits of Kieran to snuggle up tighter to, and Kieran gave the occasional hiccup). My bum was soaking wet, to match the rest of me, and Kieran looked like a Drowned Rat (though I hate to think of rats drowning, because Horace, my now elderly rat, is a Very Dear Friend). Kieran's hand felt very, very cold.

After a while Kieran leaned against me so I put my head on his shoulder. It felt comfortable there, just like in the old days when we were both *soooo* in love - except wetter, of course. Molly washed both our faces and stretched out across our laps. I looked up to ask Kieran if he was okay just as he bent his head down. It was kind of inevitable that our lips would meet, and I have to confess (again!) that it brought back all the squishy, heart-stopping feelings that I thought had gone forever.

After a long time we both moved back and laughed in an

embarrassed sort of way.

"Sorry Lainey," he mumbled. "I shouldn't have done that."

I let go of his hand, wriggled around to move Molly off, and struggled to my feet, clicking my tongue at Molly so that she'd follow me as I backed away. Kieran stood up, too, and gave me a sad smile.

"Thanks Lainey. You're a good friend," he muttered, and walked away, fast, in the direction of his house.

I picked up Molly's leash and headed for home with my head spinning like that child in the Exorcist (which I'm not allowed to watch, but did, at my best friend Amy's house). All I could think was: *Ohmygod*, I am a love rat!!! *Ohmygod*, I still have *very inappropriate* feelings for Kieran Kamau! He is still the BOMD and that is *not good*!

As we trudged past the pond Molly decided to dive in and go for a swim, dragging me with her. The fish didn't look impressed by the unexpected company and I found a clump of pondweed in my hair when we finally squelched our way through the front door. The WOD (Word of the Day) on the post-it note that Mum had stuck on the hall mirror was Scintillating. I looked at my dripping hair with its green gooey garnish and thought 'Must try harder.' It seemed fitting that I was having the worst BHD of my life after kissing Kieran, considering how many of those I'd had while we were going out together.

Mum and Dom were out, which was a relief because (a) I wouldn't feel tempted to blurt out my indiscretion and (b) it gets boring seeing your mother blowing kisses and giggling all the time. Still, there's been no mention of Ivy House for ages now, thank goodness. I've sworn on Molly and Horace's heads (which are very, very precious and beautiful) that if they ever go back there, it'll be without me.

Only after I'd towel-dried Molly, taken a hot shower, and curled up in front of the TV with a mug of Hot Chocolate and a very guilty conscience did it strike me. Kieran was always, always out gigging or doing TV shows with Dark Matter every weekend. Why was he at home?

CHAPTER 2

KIERAN

It was a mistake, I know. I shouldn't have kissed Lainey. For one thing, I'm a total mess lately and prone to doing things that have unfortunate consequences. For another, it's taken a lot for us to be friends again after I was stupid enough to get caught up in the whole fame scene and then treated her so badly. And, point three, she's in a relationship with Nat Simpson, who's a bit boring but a good guy at heart, and they seem to be happy. God knows, she deserves that, after all she's been through over the past couple of years.

Thomas, aka my father, was in his study when I arrived home and dripped my way through to the kitchen to pour a sneaky glass of whiskey. My hand shook when I picked up the bottle, and I put it down to the fact that I was frozen to the core. Thomas called through to ask if I was okay. I shouted 'Fine,' took the glass and bottle up to my room, changed into dry clothes, sat on the bed and sank two glasses in about twenty seconds. That's the tenor of our father-son relationship nowadays. Thomas works non-stop, I stay in my room most of the time I'm home, and we forage for whatever food is in the fridge when we're hungry, or order a takeaway and eat it in uncomfortable silence.

He tries hard. He really does. But since Estelle, my mother, died last year, the heart and soul has gone out of both of us and out of the house. She was such a vibrant, loving person, and I still can't believe I won't walk through the door to find her in the kitchen, baking something amazing and smiling her luminous smile. She would light up a room just by walking into it. Thomas writes to escape into his own world. I coped for a while by writing songs, but even that isn't working lately. I feel dead inside. The thought of performing on stage makes me want to run as far away as possible – to jump on a plane to Bermuda, or Iceland, or any place where no-one knows my name. It all feels so meaningless.

Lainey. It's hard to stop thinking about her. Regret is a pointless emotion, but I do regret what happened. The press made a huge deal out of all my shenanigans with other girls after Dahlia Dean, but the truth is that I wasn't really interested in any of them. It was all for show, part of the band thing that was expected of me. That doesn't make me feel good either, because they were all so pleased to be seen out with me, though they were going out with an image, a facsimile, not a real person.

I've been trying to get out of my contract with Dark Matter, but it's all sewn up so tightly that it's impossible. They've given me some time off before the next tour to get my head together, so I need to focus. Another glass of whiskey will help.

CHAPTER 3

LAINEY

It's official. I have a boyfriend (and it's not Kieran, of course). His name is Nat. Now, I have to make one thing very, very clear. Nat is not one of the boys who pursued me after Kieran dumped me via the *Tween Dreaming* photo of him and Dahlia Dean canoodling above the caption of *The Perfect Couple - New Love for Kieran*. That resulted in my Abject Public Humiliation. Not going out with any of those boys was one of the few sensible things I've ever done. Plus, I was a total screw-up for a while afterwards, and the press have plenty of photographic evidence of that extremely trying time. No, Nat just likes me for myself. Well, to be honest, it was the instant love affair between my Molly and Nat's black Greyhound, Sam, which started it off. I mean, if your dogs are acting as if they're soul-mates, you can hardly refuse them access to each other!

Nat is seventeen; a year older than me. He's tall (which is fortunate, because I'm still the second-tallest girl at school - Lucy Belling once again gets the prize for being the tallest and has grown yet another inch!). Nat has shortish dark hair that flops over his forehead, with a cute sticky-up wispy bit on top that reminds me of a Spaniel. And, carrying on with the dog theme (sorry, but I do love dogs!), he's very Spaniel-like. By that, I mean he's friendly, faithful, and absolutely brilliant at catching anything you throw at him. I've tested that out loads and he's never, ever failed. Though I think if he knew about my lapse of faithfulness with Kieran, then that would mark the end of a very happy relationship.

I'd seen him around occasionally because he's friends with

Scotty Mayhew, who thinks he's the luckiest man in history because he's going out with Amy, my best friend, and she's easily the nicest person the world has ever seen. Scotty had a huge crush on Amy for ages before she finally accepted that urban charmer John Carter was too busy working his way through all the other available (and even unavailable) girls to even notice her. So, in Scotty's case, patience paid off when Amy woke up from her John Carter-induced fantasy and realised that a Good Man had been waiting in the wings all along. But Nat and I only got talking when we bumped into each other in Victoria Park and Molly and Sam made it clear that they were in love. After that, we met up every morning to walk the dogs together before school, and the romance between Molly and Sam somehow rubbed off on us, too.

Okay, I admit it. Nat doesn't inspire the heart-stopping feeling of having my entire brain splattered all over the cosmos every time I look at him, like Kieran used to (and like he did during the brief moment of love rattiness that I'd just succumbed to). However, there are distinct advantages to this. I can have a full conversation with him without wanting to glue my lips to his (though it's very, very nice when he does kiss me), and it's a relief to not feel as if I have to physically fight off every other girl in the world. It's also a relief to be off the radar of the Paparazzi who used to sneak around after me photographing all my BHDs. Fortunately, Nat doesn't have the same magnetic effect on everyone as Kieran does, which makes for a far less stressful life. We get on really, really well, even though I know I've already met (and lost) my Soul Mate - unlike Molly and Sam, who don't waste time thinking about the past or the future. It must be quite nice to be a dog. Being with Nat after Kieran is like putting on big fluffy, comfy slippers after months of trying to dance very painfully in stiletto heels. I think I've matured since my heart was broken, because I'm taking life as it comes. Or rather, I *was*. I'm not so sure now.

Nat is not a musician. That's a huge bonus point in my book, though it was wonderful when Dark Matter won Teen Star with Kieran singing a song he'd written for me. It's not so great when your heart is broken and every radio station is playing That Song all the time. No, Nat is very sweet and thoughtful, easy-going, has no desire for fame, and his only obvious talent (apart from being incredibly nice) is that he's a genius on anything to do with computers and electrical gadgets. Maybe that makes him sound boring when you compare him with Kieran, but he really isn't and I've had quite enough of drama over the past year, thank you!

It was hard to concentrate on the TV, so I channel-hopped and worried for a while about Kieran, who shouldn't have been in Bath at all, let alone crying all alone in the park. Then I convinced myself that he was just having a bad day and that his dad, the lovely Thomas, would do whatever dads do when their offspring are upset. Not that I know anything about that first-hand, as my dad is a Love Rat of the highest order and is only interested in his second wife and her revolting child, Ian the Terrible. I also worried about whether or not I should tell Amy about my significant slip in morality. No way would I tell anyone but her. Amy is a very good person and would not approve, and that in itself would keep me on the straight and narrow path I was busy carving out for myself.

Nat phoned when I'd inadvertently chewed off the side of one fingernail. I jumped when I saw his name flash up on the screen. Did he know already? Do boys have some strange invisible antennae that picks up infidelity?

"Fancy a romantic walk in the rain with the dogs, Lainey? I'm just about to take Sam out."

Considering I'd been harbouring romantic thoughts about another, had already been thoroughly soaked, and I'd just warmed up, I politely declined but suggested they came here afterwards. Nat sounded perfectly normal so I decided not to mention Kieran, even to Amy, and to live with my guilt in silence.

CHAPTER 4

KIERAN

There's something special about a guitar. It's like a channel for all those emotions we don't quite know how to contain or express. When you're happy you can make it sing out all that joy, and it thrums against you like a living being. When you're sad, it pours out notes that flow like tears, especially if you hold a single note and let it vibrate on and on.

I haven't touched my favourite guitar, a Gibson Les Paul I'd coveted and bought with my share of our recording contract, for a week, but I lifted it off its stand, hooked the strap across, switched on the amp and stood foursquare for a minute, just feeling its weight. I slid my finger down the top E string to the twelfth fret and held it there, vibrating it. Then I put my foot on the wah wah pedal and accelerated the vibration so that it went on and on. My fingers took on a life of their own and ran up and down the frets. No chords, just notes. The room hummed around me.

I can do this when it's just me here. Now I have to find a way to do it on stage again.

Lainey's song, the first one I wrote for her, the song that paved the way to fame and fortune, flowed naturally from all those notes. She would hate to hear this now. It brings back too many memories for her. For me, though, it's the sound of love, of hope and comfort, of that wish we had at the time for a long, bright future together. I blew it, but the song brings back the best of times for me. Estelle humming it while I practiced, the pride on her face and on Thomas's when we won the Teen Star competition, Lainey's astounded expression the first time I played it to her, right here in this room, and told her I'd written it for her. That song brought about our first kiss. It's the best song I've ever written. I took a deep breath and sang it all the way through, putting my heart and soul into it.

Only when I finished did I realise my face was wet.

I put the Gibson back on its stand and wiped my eyes. Thomas was moving around downstairs, and I briefly thought about going down, too, but couldn't face an abortive attempt at conversation. He called up "That was beautiful" and I shouted "Thanks" and sat on the bed. The empty whiskey bottle rolled against my foot and I kicked it away.

CHAPTER 5

LAINEY

There aren't many things that are nicer than snuggling up in front of the fire with your boyfriend, with two large full-bellied hounds curled around each other, fast asleep beside you. Well, there are probably lots of things that are just as good, depending on what constitutes sheer bliss to you. Shopping maybe, or hang-gliding, or going on a date with the most beautiful boy in the world (Kieran Kamau). But on that particular day, with the rain beating a rhythm against the windows and a warm boy's arms around me, honing our kissing techniques (and yes, thank you, they've developed to near-perfection now), all was well in my world and I'd shifted my guilt to one of the dark recesses in my overloaded mind. It was only a kiss, after all – just a comfort kiss from a friend who's having a hard time. There was nothing in it, really. Then we heard the front door slam, and the Word Magpie (Mum) came trip-tripping through with Dom close behind her.

We quickly moved apart, trying to look as if all we'd been doing was gazing into the flames, but unfortunately mothers (even not very good ones, like Mum) have a sixth sense and always, always know they've caught their daughters with the *orbicularis oris* muscles in contraction. (That's the real term for kissing – I learned it in Biology and it somehow takes a little of the romance away, don't you think?)

"Oh! Have we interrupted something?" Mum asked, all pleased surprise. She was delighted when I hauled my emotionally traumatised self back onto to its feet and started going out with Nat.

It took the pressure off her having to look sympathetic and make lots of Hot Chocolate, and I could tell by then that she'd become very, very bored with having a Needy Daughter. Really, all Mum wants is to slope off with Dom to exotic places and canoodle, uninterrupted, to her heart's content, and they can't afford to do that yet. At least their jewellery business (you wouldn't believe what can be made out of old cutlery!) is doing well enough for us to be able to stay in our home. I still have nightmares about Ivy House and dread the moment when she says we can't afford to stay in Bath and have to go back there – not that I would. I've arranged with Amy and her parents that I can stay with them if a Dire Emergency (DM) arises, and as they saw Ivy House for themselves when they rescued me from a fate worse than death there, any possibility of future excursions in that direction would count as a First Degree DM.

Mum plonked herself down on the sofa beside us, forcing us to shuffle further along, and Dom perched on the arm and kissed the top of her head. Really, it's quite disgusting how some adults carry on! Molly and Sam raised their heads, thumped their tails vigorously, then went back to sleep. Mum subjected us to the usual questions: How was your day? Did you get soaked? Have you done your homework? And Nat, would you like to stay for dinner?

Now, Mum is a very good cook, if you like vegetarian food, though she did cook and eat flesh at Ivy House, because she gave in to peer pressure. I rebelled and nearly starved to the point of extinction. When chickpeas are involved the meals really are amazing. They take a long time to make because she removes the skins from the chickpeas first, and I've got into the habit of doing that, too, because it turns out it's quite a relaxing occupation. Tonight nut roast was on the menu. It's one of my favourites, but Nat doesn't think a meal is real food unless some poor creature has sacrificed its life. Nat swiftly told Mum that he was taking me to Bonghi Bo's and we left, pausing only to kiss Molly and Sam goodbye. At least Sam always has permission to stay at our house until Nat brings me home. Mum likes dogs just as much as I do, and she gets quite sentimental over how deeply our hounds have bonded.

Bonghi Bo's does really, really good food (I highly recommend the noodles), but it's a bittersweet place for me, because that's where Kieran took me on our first date. Nat doesn't know that, of course, and I wouldn't tell him. It's just a cool place to be, and loads of our friends go there.

We put our wet coats back on, left Mum and Dom wrapped up in each other and headed back out into the rain, with no idea of what was waiting for us there. As I said earlier, it was all the rain's fault and I really, really should have stayed at home that day.

CHAPTER 6

KIERAN

I went for a walk today, just to get out of the house. My phone had been switched off all week, and when I turned it on this morning there were texts and voicemails from the band, Dave, our manager, and a charity who wanted me to donate my body for an evening out with the winner of their auction as part of a fundraising drive. I mean, my God, the prospect of making conversation with anyone, let alone a stranger, is seriously scary right now! I switched the phone off again without returning the calls, and hid it under the bed with the growing pile of whiskey bottles.

Going out involves tying my hair back and wearing a woollen hat, black hoody, ripped jeans and dark glasses. People recognise me, otherwise, and want to stop to talk. I've learned to slouch so that I look shorter, and that combination makes me look more like a vagrant than a pop star. It works – people make a point of *not* looking at me, and I can go on my way undisturbed. I could probably get away with sitting on the ground outside Sainsbury's in Green Park and everyone would just walk on past, as they do with the homeless people who go there. Not that I just walk past them. I always drop money in the hat or cloth, because it must be awful to not have a home.

Victoria Park is a special place for me. Most people just notice the big play area that fronts onto the main road, but behind that are the Botanical Gardens and the Great Dell, which is my favourite place in Bath. There's a huge tree carving of a Green Man-type figure in the Gardens, and if you take some food and sit still for

15

long enough you may be lucky enough to have doves fly in and land on you. That's where Lainey and Molly found me on the day I went to pieces in the rain.

I went to the Dell and sat under a tree at the bottom of the hollow. Hardly anyone seems to go there, because the favoured areas have the more obvious charms of rare trees, the golf course, the skate-park and swings. It feels very peaceful. I could hear the shouts and screams of children playing, but those were overlaid by the breeze rustling through the trees and I listened to that, instead. It had a rhythm and music all of its own.

The grass was damp, but after a while I lay on my back and looked up through the branches. They made moving patterns against the sky, and that, combined with the clouds drifting past, created a beautiful kaleidoscope of shifting browns, greens and greys that I could feel myself lifting towards as if my body was floating. I let my gaze go out of focus and just watched nature's show. For the first time in months I felt peaceful and light, so when I heard someone say my name I scrambled to my feet in shock, my heart drumming out a fast tattoo.

Dianne. That sinking feeling. I'd heard how mean she'd been to Lainey when I publicly dumped her without even doing her the courtesy of telling her first. I'd never trusted Diane, there was something sort of feral about her, and if anyone who knew me was likely to talk to the press it would be her. I fixed a smile on my face.

"Shouldn't you be at school?" I asked.

She moved closer, her big eyes shining. "Nah. Bunked off. Shouldn't you be off touring all the corners of the globe?"

Despite the snippy words, her tone was flirtatious and I suppressed a shudder. I brushed mud and leaves off my jeans, trying not to look directly at her, and turned away.

"Having a brief holiday. I've got to go," I told her.

I could hear the smirk in her voice. "Important people to do and things to see?" she said. "I could come with you."

"Thanks, but I have to get on," I muttered.

Dianne stepped forward and put her hand on my arm, fluttering her lashes when I glanced sideways at her. "Well, any time you

16

need company ….." The message was clear.

"No, thank you." I shrugged her off and walked off without saying goodbye. As I turned the corner into the park I heard her laughing.

On the way home I called in at Sainsbury's and bought some ready meals and two bottles of whiskey. At the checkout I showed my fake ID (it's amazing what people will get for you when you're famous) and got through without any questions.

Thomas was out, for a change, and the house was eerily quiet. I put most of the food in the fridge, slid a lasagne into the microwave we'd bought after Estelle died (she would be horrified at the mere thought, but Thomas and I couldn't face cooking), and switched it on. During the time it took to ping to let me know the food was ready, I'd thrown back two large tumblers of whiskey. It should have made me feel better – it usually worked to at least numb me a little – but instead it hit my stomach like lead.

I took the lasagne and whiskey upstairs and sat cross-legged on my bed to eat, then reached under the bed for my phone. More messages showed as soon as I switched it on but I ignored them. Instead I started to text Lainey to tell her to be careful. I had a bad feeling about Dianne. Partway through I stopped, deleted the text and switched the phone off again. She had her own life now, I wasn't part of it, and it wouldn't be fair to step in and screw that up again.

CHAPTER 7

LAINEY

Now, those of you who already know me may remember that Dianne used to be a good friend, when she wasn't being snide. That came to an end when she got jealous about me going out with Kieran, especially once fame struck him like a lightning bolt. She was the person who let me know of the BOMDs newly minted Love Rat status. Now, you may be thinking at this point that Telling All was an act of kindness on Dianne's part – I mean, it's horrible knowing your friend is being cheated on, isn't it, and surely it's better to tell her before the paparazzi descends? But seriously, making sure I saw the photo of Kieran and Dahlia Dean on the front page of *Tween Dreaming*, then gloating about it, is not an act of friendship.

There's nothing quite as hurtful as feeling betrayed by your friend as well as your boyfriend, and I avoid her whenever possible, though that's not easy when you're at school together. However. Since Kieran dumped me, Estelle died, and my Mum moved back to Bath, I've made a point of actually turning up at school regularly *and* doing my homework. This means that as well as excelling at art, the teachers have stopped writing "Lainey is not fulfilling her potential" in my reports for everything else, it looks as if I may pass most of my GCSEs instead of coming bottom in almost everything, and it also means that I was moved to a higher group, so Dianne and I aren't in classes together, thank goodness. Scotty, Amy's boyfriend, is Dianne's brother, but fortunately she prefers to avoid her siblings when possible (we call them the Hordes because there are rather a lot of them) so that doesn't cause problems.

But Bonghi Bo's is a gathering place for all of us, and even though it was less crowded than usual, there she was by the window near the counter. And you won't believe this (I was stunned!), but she was draped all over John Carter, Love Rat of the highest order (if there was a gold medal for Love Rats, it would undoubtedly be awarded to him!) and looking very, very pleased with herself. The sight of John Carter appearing to be welcoming Dianne's lascivious attentions was even more of a shock!

Dianne is the last person I would have expected John Carter to be interested in because she's not exactly glamorous, but as he's already gone out with all the available (and some previously attached) girls in our year, the year below, the year above (and I heard a rumour that he was actually spotted snogging a very, very mature woman), maybe he's run out of options. He's good looking, in a medium height, smooth, blond, tailored dummy sort of way, though fortunately he's not my type at all (as you may have noticed, I seem to be attracted to tall, dark men), but he seems to charm his way into an awful lot of short-lived relationships. Maybe they all think they'll be the one to change his debonair ways.

She ignored me, but called out hello to Nat and then made a big deal of kissing John Carter. You could actually see their tongues – yuck! It almost put me off ordering noodles, so I walked as far over the other side as possible, Nat strolling behind me, and spotted Amy and Scotty tucked away in the corner seat, talking very animatedly. Nat and I slid behind the table to sit next to them.

"Did you see?" I whispered to Amy, sliding my eyes across to Dianne and John Carter. Amy nodded emphatically and made the sign of the zip across her lips because Scotty was right beside her. She mouthed "Later" silently, and winked.

Scotty, like Nat, is a geek, in the nicest possible way, and within nanoseconds they were both talking about incomprehensible stuff to do with gigabytes and gaming, totally forgetting we were even there. That conveniently left Amy and me free to gossip.

It turned out that Dianne and John Carter have been an item since last weekend, when he got drunk at Rosa's and Dianne saw an opportunity and leaped at it – or rather, at him – and has stuck to his side like a burr ever since. I couldn't help feeling that maybe John Carter had bitten off more than he could chew this time.

The gossip over, Amy suggested we get together for a makeover tomorrow afternoon. I eagerly agreed and then hesitated, thinking I may be just *too* tempted to tell her about my little lapse with the BOMD. Amy is a very sensitive soul, I swear she's psychic, and somehow she knew, just *knew* that I was hiding something.

"Are you okay, Lainey?" she asked.

"Oh, um, yes," I said. To my horror I felt my face get hot.

"You're blushing," Any remarked helpfully. "What have you done?"

I looked away, trying to avoid the area where Dianne and John Carter were still exercising their *orbicularis oris* muscles.

"Spill it," hissed Amy. "You only blush when (a) you've told a lie and (b) in the presence of Kieran Kamau."

It's great to have a friend who can see into your very soul, but not so good when you want to hide what's lurking around in the depths like some weird prehistoric fish. I sighed.

"Tomorrow," I told her, my heart sinking to the earth's core. It's impossible to keep a secret from Amy.

Fortunately for me, Scotty put his arm around Amy's shoulder at that point and asked if she wanted another orange juice. Nat went with him to get noodles for both of us (meaty ones for him, of course) and I managed to turn the conversation quickly to my Mum and Dom, and the amazing necklace they'd made that morning for their new Etsy shop. Amy looked suspicious but didn't pester for more information. I told you she was nice!

Mum and Dom were out in the garden shed (their studio) when we arrived back home, and Sam and Molly were soooo pleased to see us that they covered us in doggy kisses and danced around, bumping into each other and giving each other kisses, too. I went upstairs to check on Horace, who was fast asleep in his cage in my bedroom, and Nat and I curled up on the sofa together and watched television until he had to leave. It was snuggly and cosy, and I promise that I hardly thought about Kieran Kamau at all.

CHAPTER 8

KIERAN

Freddie caught me out today. He rang the landline and Thomas answered and insisted I came downstairs and spoke to him. There was a hissed, very brief argument, with me saying I didn't want to, Thomas replying that I owed it to my band to keep in touch, and ended with Thomas pushing the phone at me and walking off. The phone dropped to the floor with a clatter, the door of Thomas's study slammed, and I bent down and picked up the phone, hoping the connection had been lost. It hadn't.

After a couple of minutes of Freddie chatting away about a photo-shoot he'd just done, he cut to the point of the call.

"You are coming back next week, aren't you? We're touring Germany from Thursday."

My insides turned to ice.

"Kieran, are you there?"

Freddie is one of my closest friends in London, where we lived before moving to Bath. I've known him most of my life and we've been making music together since we were big enough to hold a full-sized instrument – he plays lead guitar and he's good, with potential to be among the best. Physically we're opposites. Freddie's short and blonde, where I'm tall and dark. We both grew up confident in our ability to do something special with our lives, and nothing had changed for him other than that he was thrilled to be living the life we'd both dreamed of. For me, everything had changed.

"Kieran?"

"Yes," I said. "I'll be there on Wednesday." We could get by without rehearsing. We all knew the songs inside out.

"Don't you want to come earlier and practice?"

"No need." I knew my voice was abrupt, but I couldn't help it. Dread seeped through like a black cloud.

"Look, Kieran, are you okay? We're worried about you. You haven't responded to calls, everyone's trying to get in touch with you ...."

"I'm fine. Gotta go. See you Wednesday." I hung up without saying goodbye and stood for a moment, leaning against the reassuring solidity of the wall. The door to Thomas's study remained closed. I stared at it, wanting to walk through it, to talk to him, to have that old, easy relationship we used to have before, in another life when we were a family. Instead, I straightened my back and went upstairs.

CHAPTER 9

LAINEY

Amy lives near me, which is handy because I spend nearly all my school-free, Nat-free time with her. In fact, now I'm doing so well at school, I even spend my school time with her. Neither of Amy's parents are Love Rats, so she lives with both of them. I used to think they were a bit stuffy until the Ivy House debacle, but they were so kind to me, letting me live with them until Mum came to her senses and returned to Bath, that I really, really love them now. I made sure they wouldn't regret taking me in by doing as much housework as I could (they're both high fliers and work long hours), and now they always call me their favourite housekeeper. It makes me laugh, because I'm one of the untidiest people in the world at home, as Amy and Mum will testify.

Usually my feet take on a special rhythm when I go to Amy's. It's a hoppity-skippety tap-tap-tap because I always, always know we're going to have fun. This time, though, I found my feet were moving more slowly than usual. It was more of a tap-tap-scuff, as if my feet already knew I was going to be in Big Trouble. Well, of course they knew, because they were attached to the rest of me, driven by messages from my brain – which was definitely aware that Amy would winkle out my deepest, darkest secret and would thoroughly disapprove of my less than honourable behaviour the day before. I almost listened to my feet and turned them in another direction, but I kept going, with Amy's house getting closer with each step.

Amy's mum answered the door. Well, she was on her way out,

and opened it as I raised my hand to knock. She looked pleased to see me and called out "Lainey's here!" then touched me gently on the shoulder as she walked past and I went inside. Amy's head appeared over the bannister at the top of the stairs, hair trailing down over the polished wood, and then the rest of her emerged as she ran down to hug me.

Now, in case you don't know Amy, I should say here that she's beautiful in a long-curly-blonde-haired, fairy-like way. The Pre-Raphaelite painters would have wanted her to be their Muse. She's small and fair and dainty, where I'm tall and reddish and lanky. We're opposites, and I suppose you could say we complement each other. Amy always has gorgeous clothes and all the new makeup and hair stuff – partly because her parents both earn a lot of money, and partly because I think they feel a bit guilty that they're not at home much. Amy used to come to my house every day after school, but now we're sixteen she goes home sometimes, or goes out with Scotty – though not often to Scotty's house because of the Hordes of children there. She's kind and caring, where I'm a bit self-obsessed. That's what Mum says, anyway, but who is she to talk? She let me languish in the hell of Ivy House, tormented by the Dorm Demons, while she sneaked off to canoodle with Dom at every opportunity and forgot all about me! Anyway, Amy and I have been best friends since we were very small, and she's never called me self-obsessed.

We collected a cola each from the fridge (I'm not allowed anything like that at home) and went up to Amy's room. Her makeup was spread out over the bed, with every colour of eye shadow and lipstick imaginable, all graded according to shade, plus blushers, shine-free face makeup, light-reflecting makeup, shimmery powder, mascaras and eye pencils. And, to my delight, her hair-straighteners. Mum won't let me use those in case I ruin my hair, so Amy always does it for me.

We sat on the floor, discussed the look of the day and decided on pale and vampy, with just a tiny smidgeon of blusher, bluish eye shadow and mascara, dark red lips, and some sparkly powder dusted over our faces afterwards. I did Amy's face first, then she did mine, and I sat cross-legged in front of her tall bedroom mirror while she knelt behind me and straightened my hair. Just as I was slipping into a hypnotic trance, watching through half-shut eyes as Amy's straighteners slid down to the floor (my hair is all the way down to my hips now, and is Mum's pride and joy, hence her disapproval of anything that could ruin it), Amy caught me unawares.

"So what have you done?" she asked in a sing-song voice.

That woke me up. I sat up straighter.

"Nothing," I said defensively.

"Oh, come on Lainey. I know you better than that. And look, you're blushing!"

You know that awful feeling when you just know you should keep your mouth shut and your secrets hidden, but somehow your mouth opens of its own accord and everything pours out? Well, that's what happened. All of it – even the kiss. I just couldn't seem to stop!

Amy's response was silence. I looked up and met her eyes in the mirror, and I swear there were tears in them. She looked totally shocked.

"Lainey, I am totally shocked," she said, moving the straighteners away from my hair (and it was only half-done!) and putting them down on their stand. She sat on the floor and turned me around by the shoulders so that I was facing her instead of the mirror. I didn't need to look – I could feel my face burning.

"It wasn't anything," I protested. "It just happened, and it won't happen again."

Amy looked fierce. She's a very honest person, and I could see that my being a Love Rat hadn't done me any favours in her opinion of me at all. I hung my head but she raised my chin and made me look right at her before starting that horrible ticking off of fingers thing that people do when you really are in trouble with them.

"You. Are. In. A. Relationship. With. A. Really. Nice. Boy. Who Cares. About. You." A finger was ticked off with each word. I started to open my mouth but she glared at me so I closed it again.

"Kieran. Is. A Love. Rat. Who. Dumped. You. Publicly. Via. *Tween. Dreaming.* Magazine."

"I know, I ....."

"Be quiet! You. Will. Totally. Screw. Up. Your. Life. If. You. Take. This. Any. Further."

I took both of Amy's hands in mine to stop her ticking off any more words. It was starting to irritate me to the point where the shame I felt faded into the background.

"Listen! It didn't mean anything!" I shouted. "It was raining. He was upset. He lost his mum, for goodness sake, and is followed everywhere he goes by vultures wanting front page spreads out of him! It was only one little kiss and we went our separate ways!"

Amy's shoulders relaxed. "Okay, I believe you," she said quietly, "But please don't go hurting Nat. He really, really likes you."

"And I really, really like him," I told her. "He's my comfy slippers."

Amy's beautifully shaped and darkened eyebrows rose.

"I mean, he's comfortable to be with. I can just enjoy being with him without having to try to be glamorous," I explained. "I'd far rather be with Nat." Okay, I crossed my fingers behind my back as I said that, hoping Amy wouldn't see them in the mirror. Fortunately, she didn't.

That seemed to work. Amy hugged me and apologised for getting so upset and angry. I accepted her apology and then apologised to her for being such an idiot. She finished my hair. I straightened her hair. We had toast and honey followed by chocolate cake, and talked about Scotty's new-found talent on the decks (he aspires to be a Dj), and everything returned to normal.

It was only when I was back home, tucked into bed with Horace nibbling the sheets by my feet in his favourite ratty occupation, that I admitted it to myself. I was still in love with Kieran Kamau and nothing, but *nothing*, was ever going to come of it.

CHAPTER 10

KIERAN

On the road again. It may sound glamorous, but it's not. We have a really cool van, like a large camper, that we travel in, often sleep in (if we're lucky we get hotel rooms some nights), and hang out in, and by day three it smells of sweaty socks and stale curry, and is a mess of clothes, instruments, take-out cartons and boxes, and other things it's best I don't go into. Put four men (well, male teenagers) in one cramped place for weeks on end and the most harmonious relationships turn sour. We need breaks between tours so that, as well as resting (or partying), song-writing and rehearsing, we can rebuild the friendships that brought us together in the first place. Up until Estelle died I loved the life.

I try to learn a few words of the language of each country we tour, so that I can greet the audience. Sometimes it's backfired because of my pronunciation. In Poland, I thought I was saying "Please," which is *proszę*, but after the audience dissolved into hysterics I discovered I'd said *prosiaczek*, which means 'piglet.' That took a while to live down, and for months the rest of the band made snorting noises every time I said "please" to anyone. I laughed as much as they did.

It was only when we piled into the first venue and watched the roadies setting up that I realised I hadn't got around to learning any German. I'd been hoping not to be here at all. That's when I knew I had to shape up and get into the spirit of the tour, otherwise I'd ruin it for everyone. I listened for an accent and went over to a guy in the wings to ask him how to introduce the band, and to check my pronunciation. After writing it down phonetically and repeating it a few times, I came close enough to be understandable.

The first few gigs went well, and the parties afterwards were wild, with floor to ceiling girls and rivers of booze. Each night I let a few of them kiss me, drank myself into a stupour, and Chris, the drummer and the strongest of all of us, hauled me back to the van to sleep it off and then returned to partying. Each morning I woke with a headache and a sick feeling in my stomach, and by the final gig it seemed the only way to get through it was to have a few whiskies before going on-stage.

That was not my finest couple of hours.

The awful moment when I knew I'd had one drink too many came partway through the first song, when my balance went off-kilter and my voice started to slur. I finished the song, caught the dirty looks that Freddie, Mike and Chris were directing my way, and stepped back to let Freddie introduce the next song with a story while I guzzled down large quantities of water to try and sober up.

Of course, all that fluid meant that I was bursting for the loo halfway through. I casually strolled over to Freddie and muttered that I needed him to do a guitar solo so I could get offstage for a couple of minutes to pee. Freddie glared at me and moved to the front of the stage, mouthing "Solo" at Chris and Mike, and I exited stage left, begged for something to pee in, and had the indignity of being offered a large beer tankard. It had to do. I just prayed it wouldn't end up on eBay or anything. Oh, the shame.

After the gig I really caught it in the ear from the others, which was fair enough. I went straight to bed and missed the final party, which got me in even more trouble because someone from a big radio show was there, interviewing the band, and the lead singer was missing. Some excuse was made that I had a bug, which avoided any really bad press, but Chris, our drummer, gave me hell the next morning. I stared at the floor while he ranted about responsibility, commitment, and how I'd better get my act together, pronto. My lack of response made him even madder.

"Look at me." He poked me in the chest hard enough to knock me off balance. I looked.

Chris is shorter than me, heavy-set and stocky, with long, straight black hair and biceps that a wrestler would be proud of from all that drumming. His blue eyes were like chips of ice.

"Sorry," I mumbled.

Chris glared. "You pull that stunt again and you'll be more than sorry, mate," he roared, and stalked off.

Freddie and Mike, our lead guitarist, glanced sideways at me and followed him. I sat on the rumpled duvet and felt totally, utterly lost.

CHAPTER 11

LAINEY

My mum has two sisters and a brother. Aunt Bee is an actress, and until recently all her roles have been small ones where she mostly looked very bedraggled. But her last role was a leading one at last, in a biopic called *A Woman in Eden*. She played Marianne North, a Victorian botanical artist who travelled all over the world painting flowers, and whose paintings are still exhibited at the Royal Botanic Gardens at Kew. I can see why Aunt Bee got so into 'being Marianne' as she put it, because she has an adventurous spirit, too - and it has to be said that, as usual, she looked less than elegant through much of the film, even though she was the star. She bought me a book about Marianne called *Vision of Eden* and that really sparked off my interest in painting and got me into collecting other books about art and doing loads of experimenting. Up until then I'd been primarily known for my caricatures, and most of those got me into trouble at school (that's what happens when you draw caricatures of your teachers!) but I bought myself some oil and watercolour paints and discovered that I was really quite good at painting, as well as drawing.

Anyway. The film was based on Marianne's life, but of course there had to be a love story, even though Marianne never married. Aunt Bee filmed in Australia, Hawaii, Africa and Chile, which she said was very, very exciting. And, inevitably, she fell in love with Marianne's fictional lover, called Edward Blatchley in the film, who was played by the utterly gorgeous Jack Munroe! He fell in love with her, too, and they decided to throw a party to celebrate the film getting rave reviews.

Aunt Bee and Jack have rented a farmhouse just outside Bath, near Farmborough, and lots of people were there, including the family and some of their friends from the film industry. I felt unusually glamorous in the calf-length purple velvet dress and jade green very high-heeled sandals that Aunt Bee bought me especially for the party – a special gift for getting my GCSE's over with, though I had no idea whether I'd done well. It was really funny to see Nat's jaw drop when he came round to travel in the car with me, Mum and Dom. Nat looked pretty good himself – I'd never seen him wearing a suit before!

I was a bit star-struck. I mean, Jack Munroe has been in so many of my favourite films, and I had to make a huge effort to stop staring at him even though I'd met him once already, just after filming ended. Aunt Bee is very pretty, and she looked stunning in a floor length white Grecian-style draped gown. I didn't dare go and speak to any of the Big Names there, but Aunt Bee looked perfectly relaxed and made sure she introduced me to everyone. It was nerve-wracking, and I felt quite relieved to go and sit with the family afterwards.

Mum and Dom didn't seem at all in awe of the elevated company, and Uncle Denny is so at ease with everyone that he chatted away as if he was used to being surrounded by movie stars. Perhaps he is. He's one of my favourite people. He tells great stories and makes me laugh a lot, and I've never quite figured out exactly what he does for a living. I think it's something in Public Relations, and he loves meeting new people. Aunt Carol and her husband, Uncle Todd, are very straight-laced and a bit shy. They didn't look at all comfortable – especially when Jack lifted Aunt Bee right off her feet and twirled her around before going in for a massive snog that had everyone clapping.

Nat and I sat close together, people-watching and listing the films that we'd seen various actors in. Jack popped open a *huge* bottle of champagne and everyone applauded, then women in black and white uniforms went around with trays of glasses, handing them out. Me and Nat got one each, too! The bubbles went up my nose and we both got the giggles. It didn't taste horrid, like the wine that Amy and I sometimes 'borrowed' at her house, and I drank it quickly, then went to accept another, but Aunt Carol dug me hard in the ribs and put the full glass back on the tray.

Nat asked me to dance, and I jumped up and then realised my heels were a bit too high for easy balance. My ankles kept wobbling. Nat propped me up and I wound my arms around his neck and kissed him. That brought another round of applause, but I was enjoying myself *soooo* much that I just laughed and kissed Nat again. We stumbled in and out of other people who were dancing, and then the music shifted up tempo and I took my arms from Nat's neck, caught hold of his hands and did a twirl.

Twirling in high heels when you don't usually wear them is not a good idea. My left ankle went in a different direction to my sandal, and I totally lost my balance and careened across the floor, grabbing the nearest person for safety – who happened to be Jack. Jack went over, too, knocking against Aunt Bee, who fell against Alan Forbinger, the director of the film – who bounced sideways and into A lister movie star Anya Broadstairs, who joined us all in an undignified heap on the floor. It was like human dominoes. And, to make it even worse, Anya's dress tore, revealing a long pale length of upper thigh. Everyone else laughed as they got to their feet and Nat dived in to help me up, but Anya Broadstairs was furious, even though Jack offered to buy her a new dress and Aunt Bee took her upstairs to borrow one of her outfits.

I was mortified, and all I could think about was that I'd lost a sandal somewhere in the melee. Mum and Dom were shrieking with laughter, Uncle Denny was nowhere to be seen (I heard later that he'd sloped off with one of the actresses), and Aunt Carol and Uncle Todd were absolutely livid and refused to speak to me.

Mum, in the spirit of damage control, took us home, dropping Nat off first. She thought it was hilarious, fortunately. My sandal never did turn up. And I have a sneaking feeling I won't be invited to any more A list parties.

CHAPTER 12

KIERAN

Back home for two weeks, thank goodness. Nothing had changed. Thomas and I politely stepped around each other, I went for walks in disguise, veered in a different direction if I saw anyone who vaguely resembled Dianne, and kept my eyes peeled for Lainey's tall, willowy shape. I didn't see her, but I bumped into Scotty and we talked about nothing much for a few minutes. In the end I couldn't help it, and asked whether he saw much of Lainey. He looked a bit surprised and said that she and Amy had just done their GCSE's and that Lainey and Nat got together quite often with him and Amy. It felt like a pointed comment, justifiable considering Amy had picked up the pieces after Lainey and I broke up. I pasted on a smile and said that was good, then we went our separate ways with, I'm sure, a sense of relief on both sides.

There's a guy I knew during my brief time at school here who has a reputation for being able to get anything you want. Darren isn't someone I'd normally choose to hang out with. He has older, scary friends who would tear your head off rather than smile at you, and he talks in patois, even though he's English. I met him in the park just after the uncomfortable conversation with Scotty, and he was friendly without mentioning the fame thing, which was refreshing, so we ended up sitting under the trees for a while. He rolled a joint and passed it to me. I hesitated, then took it, even though I don't smoke.

"That'll give you some creative inspiration," he said, as I inhaled and slowly blew out the smoke before coughing my guts up.

He laughed. "Keep going. It gets easier." So I did, and it did.

A whole afternoon passed in a haze of wellbeing, something I hadn't experienced for what seemed like forever. When Darren got up to leave I asked where I could buy some, and he grinned and dug into his pocket. "How much do you want?" he asked.

Back home, I opened my bedroom window, rolled a joint inexpertly, and lay back on my bed, smoking. I felt mellow, able to drift away from all the fear, and guilt, and grief. The Gibson on its stand across the room seemed to be calling me, so I stubbed out the butt on a plate and went to lift the guitar, cradling it against me like a baby. It felt warm and alive.

Sitting on the side of the bed, I picked out a few notes, then a few more. They resonated against my chest, singing to me. After repeating the riff a couple more times, I started to hum along, then to sing whatever came into my head. The song took shape, it almost seemed to be writing itself, and I grabbed the notebook by my bed and scribbled down the words while picking out notes with my left hand.

It was a sad song, of love and loss and loneliness, but hauntingly beautiful. I played it through twice and then recorded it on my phone to make sure I wouldn't forget it. Then I downloaded it onto my laptop, played it back and worked on some harmonies, and emailed the file to the rest of the band to get their feedback on it.

Freddie was the first to respond. "It's good," he wrote. "Very different to our other stuff, though. Dreamy. Wonder whether it'll work on the next album. Might not fit in." Not long afterwards Mike and Chris sent similar replies.

You know that feeling when you rise out of a very dark cloud and then fall back into it? The cloud feels even stickier and heavier than before.

I gave in to temptation and texted Lainey.

CHAPTER 13

LAINEY

You probably guessed that Kieran wouldn't just disappear, didn't you? Well, you were right. About a week after The Party (oh, the shame!!), he texted me to ask whether I would go round to his house. I went (just out of curiosity, of course!) and took Molly with me. And no, I didn't tell Nat, or Amy, or Mum. There was no need for them to know. After all, I was only seeing him as a friend.

It was a bittersweet feeling walking the old route down beside Victoria Park, being met at the door by Kieran, and following him into the house. I'd done that so many times before. Kieran did not look his best. His hair was wild and his eyes were red-tinged, but his smile was warm and genuine and he bent down to stroke Molly's soft ears. She gazed up at him adoringly. The house looked just the same as when I'd last been there, just after Estelle died, but it felt like a show house instead of a home. Estelle was always in the huge kitchen when I used to visit, cooking amazing cakes and garnishing meals with real flowers, chattering away happily in her husky voice with a French accent. The house looked pristine but soulless.

Thomas, Kieran's dad, was working in his study and stopped typing for a moment to call out hello. He's an award-winning author and his study is amazing – there's even a fountain in there! Kieran and I went into the kitchen and he peered into the fridge and brought out a carton of mango juice, pouring some into two of their beautiful crystal glasses. We sat at the table, opposite each other with Molly lying quietly at my feet, and Kieran just looked at me. I looked back, and what I saw concerned me. His spark, that sense of electricity zapping out all around him, had gone.

"Are you okay?" I asked, knowing how stupid that must sound. It was obvious he was having a hard time.

Kieran shuffled in his chair and looked away, then back at me.

"Not really," he said. "I want out."

"Out of what? Dark Matter?" I knew he'd been under huge pressure to perform, even straight after Estelle died. It must have been hell for him.

Kieran stretched an arm across the table and took my hand in his, turning it over and looking down at my palm as if it held all the answers.

"Oh Lainey, I don't know. I feel so lost and I just can't care about it anymore. What does it matter, anyway? It's just a bunch of people up on stage, getting off on all the girls screaming for them. And the parties – having to look as if you're having fun, when all you want to do is crawl off and be alone. And people wanting to know what you're wearing, and what shampoo you use, and whether you've screwed this person or that one."

I must admit, I was shocked. I mean, Kieran *loved* that lifestyle! It's what he'd dreamed of. And I didn't even want to think of him having sex. I mean, our relationship was just kissing, and the thought of all that (urgh!) *intimacy* scared me. It hurt to even thinking of him kissing someone else, which was hypocritical of me because I was going out with Nat and we did loads of kissing. But losing your mum, who just happens to be the loveliest, most caring (and beautiful) mum on the planet has to have an effect on you, doesn't it? I really was at a loss for words, so just asked whether Thomas knew how he felt. Kieran shook his head, dark ringlets flying around his face.

"Dad's struggling, too, but he channels it all into his writing."

"Have you talked to … um … a counsellor or anyone? That might help."

Kieran laughed, but there was no humour in it, and shook his head again. "No, I'm just getting on with it. It'll pass. I've got two weeks off, but we have another tour after that so I have to go back."

I stroked his hand with my thumb. "It'll get easier," I murmured.

Kieran nodded, then gave a small smile. "Will you watch a film with me? Really, I just want to be around people I trust, and you're the only one who won't go telling tales to the press."

"Of course," I said. And yes, I did feel flattered that he trusted me.

We watched an old, old favourite, *Raiders of the Lost Ark*, sitting at opposite ends of the sofa with Molly curled up between us, laughing in the same places. Afterwards I told Kieran I had to go home because I'd promised to help the Word Magpie make dinner, and he grinned and teased me about how I'd changed from the girl who would bunk off school and avoid her mother at every opportunity. He offered to walk me home, but no way could I let that happen. I'd never be able to hide it from Mum – or anyone else, for that matter – if we were seen together.

We had veggie shepherd's pie (no chickpeas) and it took me ages to get to sleep that night. I lay awake for hours, worrying about him. At two in the morning my phone pinged. It was a text from Kieran that simply read 'Thnk yu xxx.' I texted back 'Anytime xxx,' then stayed awake for even longer, thinking that was probably not a wise response.

CHAPTER 14

KIERAN

The next couple of days drifted by in a dream. I discovered that whiskey and hash combined just makes you throw up, so decided my little foray into the drug world had to end right there. At least whiskey was accessible, though still not strictly legal, considering I was still seventeen. And, three days after seeing Lainey, I realised that booze wasn't going to help in the long term. I needed to get my head together and stop feeling so sorry for myself.

That song stuck in my head, though. It was like putting a piece of me into music. Maybe it wasn't right for the band, but I could just keep it private, for my ears only, and focus on writing heavier Dark Matter tracks. I spent hours standing in the corner of the room, facing the wall to shut out all distractions (including my thoughts), trying out different riffs, and two finally came together that fitted our style. I recorded them, sent them to the guys, and had positive feedback, so I worked on them some more.

Thomas came into the kitchen when I went down to get some juice. He patted me on the shoulder as he passed me to put a mug in the sink, and suggested we get a takeaway. We ate vegetable biryani and poppadums in between making stilted conversation, like strangers, about how his new book was going.

A momentary silence seemed to suddenly drag on, and I looked up to find Thomas staring at me, his brow furrowed. He looked older, his black hair was tinged with grey around the sides, and lines had appeared on his face that I hadn't noticed before.

"What?" I knew I sounded defensive, and instantly regretted it.

"Kieran, I know it's hard," he said. "But we still have each other. We can't go on avoiding each other like this."

"I don't know what you mean."

"Yes, you do. I worry about you. You've become very …. insular."

"I just need some quiet time. It gets so crazy when we're touring," I muttered.

Thomas put his fork down and leaned forward. "Are you unhappy in the band?"

I shrugged. "It's just … intense, at the moment. I don't feel in a party mood. But it'll be okay." There was no point in burdening him. He had enough to deal with.

"I'm here if you ever feel like talking," he said quietly, and picked up his fork. We finished the meal in silence.

CHAPTER 15

LAINEY

Dinner at our house is usually a noisy affair, even with just three of us. Mum and Dom talk constantly and I tend to just tune out, so it took a moment for me to come to and realise that Mum had said my name. I looked up from my chickpea curry (very tasty), my mind still elsewhere, to find Mum's face almost touching mine. That made me jump.

"What?" I asked, a bit crossly.

"You're looking very distracted at the moment, Lainey. Is everything okay?"

As Mum doesn't usually notice anything, she really does live on a different plane to me, her sudden concern was slightly worrying. I mean, I love her and everything, because she's my mum, but she'd never win mother of the year award.

"I'm fine," I muttered, edging some stray chickpeas onto my fork.

Mum didn't look convinced. "What you need is a tarot reading," she said.

My heart sank. For one thing, I don't believe in all that stuff, even though she has a reputation for being good at it; and for another, if I did believe in it, I certainly didn't want to know what the future held. I had a feeling it may not be quite what I hoped for – you know, good hair days every day, no spots, wealth beyond measure, passing all my exams, Kieran Kamau declaring his monogamous and undying love, and Nat being delighted just to see me happy.

I shook my head. Mum leaned in even closer, took my chin in her hand, and stared into my eyes. It was freaky, so I closed them. My fork clattered against the plate as I dropped it, splattering spicy chickpeas all over my lap, so I opened my eyes and looked down at the mess on my favourite charity shop skirt. It was not pretty. Dom leaped up to get a damp dishcloth (he's amazingly domesticated) and I focussed on sponging bits of curry off my skirt.

"Come on," Mum coaxed. "It'll be fun, and you might be surprised by how accurate it is."

I wasn't sure I wanted an accurate reading. I certainly didn't want the Word Magpie to know my innermost thoughts! But I knew she'd go on and on so I followed her into the living room. She looked like Molly after she's filched cheese from the counter – very, very smug.

Mum guided me to the nearest sofa (as if I couldn't find my own way there!), dragged a side table over in front of me, and brought a dining chair through, before fetching her cards from her bedroom. She keeps them wrapped in a piece of black silk cloth in a carved box, which supposedly stops them from picking up on weird vibrations that may be floating around the house. As the weird vibes here come from her and Dom, the protective measures seemed a bit pointless to me. Mum came back down, wearing her 'mystic' necklace (made from a melted spoon, with an amethyst set in the centre – a gift from Dom), flicked her dreadlocks over her shoulder (she had such pretty fair hair before we moved to the Commune From Hell, and now it's all dreaded and ratty), sat opposite me on the dining chair and handed me the cards as if they were gold-plated and covered in precious jewels.

"Just shuffle them and ask a question in your mind," she said in the whispery sing-song voice she uses with her clients.

Now, tarot cards are bigger than ordinary playing cards, and I've never been much good at shuffling, anyway, so I dropped a couple. Mum peered at them when she bent to pick them up.

"Oooh, The Tower," she cooed, handing them back so that I could slide them into the deck again. "And the Four of Wands. Big changes are coming your way."

I'd had enough changes to last for several lifetimes, so I didn't much like the sound of that. I shuffled the cards again, slowly, making sure no more of them fell out, and then handed them over to her.

"Put them on the table, face down, and cut them into three piles, then put them back into one pile," she said. I sighed heavily but complied. I bet none of the other girls I know has to put up with all this from their mothers. Amy certainly doesn't!

Mum picked up the deck and laid out seven cards in a V shape, face down. "This is called the Bird Spread, because it's in the shape of a bird's wings," she told me. *Whatever*, I thought. *Just get this over with*. She carefully turned the cards over. I gasped. The Tower and the Four of Wands were both there. Mum smiled. "Well, there's clearly a strong message coming through for you," she murmured.

You know that feeling when every hair on your body stands on end? That was just how I felt while Mum explained the reading to me.

"Look," she said, pointing. "In your present situation you have The Lovers, which means you're being faced with a choice between your head and your heart. The present influence is the Ace of Pentacles, so it's important to stay grounded. The direction to take is the Five of Staffs, which can be an inner battle that you'll win if you stay true to yourself. The outcome is the Two of Cups, a loving relationship." She looked up at me, smiling. "Well, you know that, because you already have it."

I nodded, though doubtfully. This was scaring me. Mum carried on, touching each card as she spoke. "The unexpected influence is The Tower. That's a tricky card. It means destruction of all that's old and familiar, a bit like the phoenix rising from the ashes." I swallowed. "Help to be obtained is the Two of Swords. That's another tricky card. It can mean that you're closing your eyes, blindfolding yourself to the truth, but it can also mean that you're protecting your heart energy in order to seek inner peace. And finally, the influence of the outcome on your life is the Four of Wands, the completion of a cycle and the beginning of a new cycle. You'll be making plans and putting them into action, and it'll be an exciting time."

She leaning back, smiling. "Does that make sense to you?"

"Nope," I said abruptly, and ran up to my room, swiftly followed by Molly. Up on my bed, with the door firmly closed and Molly happily taking up most of the bed-space, I stroked her soft head and ears, and shut my eyes. The image of a falling tower engulfed in flames flashed up, so I sat up and listened to Molly's' groans of bliss as she burrowed up against me.

CHAPTER 16

KIERAN

A crashing crescendo of screaming guitars and frantic drum rhythms woke me, and I sat up, drenched in sweat and with my heart beating at double-time, to find the room silent. It must have been a dream. It took a few minutes for my breathing to steady, and then I re-ran the music in my head.

Still feeling shaky, I showered, made coffee and took a cup through to Thomas, who, as always, was at his keyboard. The tinkling of the waterfall in his writing room was soothing, and somehow slipped into an undertone for the cacophony that had hurled me into wakefulness. It gave me an idea.

"Thomas, do you mind if I record this?" I asked, putting the cup on a space among his notes. He looked up, slightly dazed, as he always is when he's immersed in a book.

"Ah, thanks. Record what, Kieran?"

"The water. It has such a soft rhythm."

"Of course. Help yourself." He smiled, and it was like seeing the sun come out. Thomas has rarely smiled since Estelle died. And yes, I use the D word. Passed away, left us, has departed – all those sugary terms for the harsh reality just made me feel angry.

I left my coffee on the corner of the desk, ran up to grab my phone, and went to sit beside the fountain while I recorded. Thomas took a sip of his coffee and handed my cup to me. We sat in silence, both lost in our thoughts. After a couple of minutes I stopped the recording and stood up.

"We could go somewhere, if you like," Thomas suggested.

"Uh, thanks, but no. I have to put some tracks together." Then I looked up. His smile had vanished, and he looked crushed. It was like a knife in my heart. "Well …." I said…

"No. No, it's fine. I have a deadline to meet. It was just a silly idea," he said hastily, and turned back to his laptop.

Oh, Guilt, I thought, as I slowly walked back upstairs, *you must be my middle name nowadays.*

I uploaded the water sounds onto my computer, opened the music programme and searched for a similar drum-beat to the one in my dream, then plugged in the Les Paul. Two hours later I played the recording back; layers of sound, two overlaid tracks of harsh screaming guitar, and heavy drums against a backdrop of rushing water. I listened closely twice, my heart beating fast, then lay back on my bed with my notepad and played it through again.

The words started to flow.

CHAPTER 17

LAINEY

They say things happen in threes (though quite who said it originally is a mystery), and that was certainly true that week. First the visit to Kieran's house, then an unpleasant altercation with Dianne, and then my very, very worst nightmare came back to haunt me.

Maybe I should back-track a bit here. You already know about Kieran, of course, and you also know that Nothing Untoward happened with him at his house so my conscience is clear. Well, apart from That Kiss in the rain that I mentioned earlier, but that was an accident and is all in the past. I've forgotten all about it, except when I think about The Lovers card in Mum's tarot deck. Dianne and I had a scuffle at school (that was the second Thing), and then Thing Number Three came out of the blue like one of Thor's thunderbolts (he was the king of the Norse gods, and ruled over thunder, among other things, in case you didn't know).

So, Dianne. Well, she walked past me just as I was getting some books out of my locker on Wednesday, and deliberately bumped into me so hard that the locker door banged against my arm. It hurt, and I squealed in pain and instinctively stepped sideways to bump her back. Everyone looked around and stopped talking as Dianne flew across the corridor and hit the opposite wall.

Unfortunately, Mr Podd, who teaches history, happened to be passing by just as Dianne made contact with the wall. He blamed me, of course. He hasn't liked me since I drew a caricature of him as a slug, not long before I was dragged off to Ivy House. I got three days of after school detention and a letter was sent to Mum. Mum is very anti-violence (and so is Dom), so I was in Deep Trouble with her, too, over the Diane Incident, and was grounded and put on washing up duty for the rest of the week. That meant four days of washing up and I was not happy.

Amy and our friend Rosie saw it happen, but when they tried to speak out on my behalf they were told that no excuses would be accepted. They were allowed round to visit me, as I could only leave the house for the walk to school and back, so for the next two schooldays we muttered dire curses on Mr Podd and Dianne at every opportunity. Nat wasn't very sympathetic when I texted him to say I wasn't allowed to walk Molly, and that Mum would be doing the exercise routine instead. He thought I should have used more self-restraint. I was so offended that I refused to let him come around while I was grounded.

When I texted the sorry tale to Kieran, he texted back an hour later, just after Amy arrived. 'D is a prat, Warrior Woman ;-) xxx'. That made me feel a bit better, until Amy asked who the text was from. "Nat," I said quickly, and blushed.

Amy dived across the room to grab my phone. "Don't tell fibs!" she said, checking my texts. "As I thought. Kieran. You said there was nothing going on with him." So I told her he'd invited me round, and we'd watched a film at opposite ends of the sofa.

"Lainey, Lainey, will you never, ever learn? You have a lovely boyfriend and Kieran is a Love Rat! In fact, *you* now qualify as a love rat, too!"

"We can still just be friends," I muttered sulkily. "For goodness sake!"

Amy sniffily pointed out that friends don't feel a need to keep their friendships secret from other friends, especially from their best friend in the whole wide world. She did have a point, but I shouldn't have to ask her permission, and I told her that.

Amy went home in the closest I've ever seen to a huff, and it took twelve apologetic texts in which I swore that I would never, ever keep a secret from her again. After the twelfth one she relented and texted back "OK, ur forgiven. But no more lies!!!" No kisses at the end, though.

What with washing up all the time (you wouldn't *believe* the mess Mum and Dom make when they're cooking!), and not seeing Nat (which was, after all, my choice – but still, he could have been more understanding), and not walking Molly (how I *love* walking Molly), and worrying about whether Kieran was going to leave Dark Matter (and what would he do without his music?), and trying to avoid Dianne's smirks every time I had to go to the hall for detention at the end of the day, I was not at my most cheerful.

Then the third Thing of the accursed Three happened, and that knocked me totally off my metaphorical feet.

CHAPTER 18

KIERAN

Week two, and I only have a few days left at home before we do some gigs in Scotland. I'm trying hard to pull myself together. As Lainey and Thomas had made a big deal about me being a mess, other people would notice, too. So, no drinking. Well, just one glass. Definitely no hash, and I stuck to that, even though I bumped into Darren and he offered me a special deal. I declined politely.

Lots of fresh fruit juice. Cooking was mostly beyond me, but I made an effort and did vegetables to go with the ready meals. I even took them through to Thomas so that he would eat better. He seemed to appreciate that. When he's writing he forgets the time, which means he often forgets to eat. Estelle used to make sure he had breaks, and they always spent evenings together, but without her here he just carried on until he couldn't see the screen any more. I knew that because if I saw him come through, late at night, he'd be rubbing his eyes and blinking like a sleepy owl.

I honed the new song and wrote some more, and sent those to Freddie, Mike and Chris. Everyone really liked the one I thought of as 'Cacophony,' but the others didn't have the fire in them that was so characteristic of my music 'before,' as I thought of it. Still, they were good enough to get the band's creative juices flowing, and their input made a difference. There was enough material for another album, and the recording company folks were rubbing their hands together and clearly seeing us in terms of more £ and $ signs. It helped keep them all happier that I was answering my mobile and returning texts now, as well.

Inside I still felt numb, except when I thought of Estelle, when my insides turned to a searing mass of pain; and when I thought of Lainey, which brought a complicated mix of regret, and guilt, and yearning. I cursed myself for being so dumb as to let her go. I had a feeling that if I talked to a counsellor they would tell me that Lainey was a symbol of my happy past and all that was once good in my life, and I was just projecting my longing to return to that onto her. But that wasn't true. Lainey was in love with Nat, or she wouldn't be with him, but she was the only person to show real compassion and sympathy. I knew she cared.

In the end I talked to Freddie when he rang to discuss the song list. He's the most sensitive of the guys in Dark Matter, he'd known me the longest, and he was honest enough to tell me to get myself in gear and move on. As he pointed out, Lainey had moved on a while ago, and was just being a good friend, that I was reading more into it because I was still struggling over Estelle's loss. It hurt to hear it, but I knew he was right.

CHAPTER 19

LAINEY

You know those days when you wish you'd just stayed in bed, as deep under the duvet as possible? I've had quite a few of those, but Sunday soon went on my list of The Worst Days of My Life.

It started off well, considering I was still grounded (my final day, thank goodness). Mum and Dom made pancakes for breakfast and were beginning to accept that I hadn't turned into a Violent Teenager who was going to go out beating people up for fun. We actually had a laugh about Mr Podd, who Mum always felt needed a sense of humour implant.

Amy came round and made it clear, without actually discussing it, that she'd forgiven me. I could tell because she brought round some makeup samples that her Mum had been given in Jolly's. Mum took Molly out for a walk, and I started washing dishes while Amy and I chatted. Then the doorbell rang.

"Dom, can you get that?" I called, thinking Mum had probably forgotten her key.

A moment later I heard a shout of surprise from Dom (so it clearly wasn't Mum) and a voice that sounded horribly familiar. My heart stopped for a moment, even while I was telling myself that it couldn't possibly, possibly be who I thought it was. I dropped the plate I was washing and sudsy water splashed all over me as it landed back in the sink. Amy saw that I'd gone white around the gills and started to ask what was wrong as Dom walked through, followed by four people I'd hoped and prayed to never, ever see again in my entire life.

I really, truly thought I was going to faint, and clutched the side of the sink for support. There, smirking, stood my Nemeses (is that the plural for Nemesis?) from Ivy House, the Commune from Hell in deepest Nottinghamshire! Four of the people who had made my life unbearable for three whole months were here, in my home.

Evil dreadlocked Sarah, who had locked me in my room for days on end. Her two vile daughters, Pixie and Bryony, who had tortured me by stealing all my belongings, including my letters from Kieran, Amy and co., tried to seduce Kieran, and ultimately almost managed to persuade me that Kieran had dumped me (the dumping came later, of course). And, lowest of the low, Creepy Lincoln, who had stared at my boobs and never met my eyes, and who'd tried to grab me in the corridor and kiss me. Gross. That was the only time I've ever been glad to see Sarah, because she came along and interrupted, which meant I could escape unscathed. The only person who'd ever been kind to me there was Aileen, and I looked behind them to see whether she was here, too, but she wasn't.

They all looked exactly the same. Scruffy, smug, and with that familiar nasty glint in their eyes when they stared at me – all except for Creepy Lincoln, whose eyes were focused further south, as usual. I pulled my cardigan tighter around me and crossed my arms over my chest.

"What are they doing here?" I asked, hating it that my voice sounded high and shaky. Just seeing them made me feel small and very scared.

Dom laughed, clearly totally unaware of how horrified I felt. "They're in the area for a few days and called in to say hello," he said cheerfully.

"Hello and goodbye," I muttered. "You can go now. You're not welcome here." And that's when Mum walked in with Molly. She didn't look thrilled. Mum is not the most sensitive person on the planet, and she was too busy canoodling with Dom to realise how cruel they all were to me until Amy's parents arrived to give her a royal talking-to and whisk me back to Bath to stay with them. She tried very, very hard to make it up to me afterwards, when she moved back to Bath with Dom in tow.

However. Mum is polite, even to people who are not nice, and she moved me out of the way to fill the kettle. Grounded or not, I got out of there with Amy and we went to her house, where I sat chewing my knuckles and hoping they'd be gone by the time I went back home. All the awful memories came flooding back and I couldn't stop shaking. Amy made Hot Chocolate and was very reassuring. When her parents came home they were shocked, too, and said I could stay with them for the night if Mum gave permission.

I rang Mum later in the evening. She said they were staying overnight, all of them in the spare room, and that I had to come home. I insisted that I'd stay with Amy but she put her foot down and said that if she had to come and get me I would be grounded for another week. I couldn't *believe* she was being so mean! I went home with my spirits somewhere in the vicinity of the Big Bang, that apocalyptic event at the beginning of the universe, and knew just how the poor BB must have felt. I swear I could feel my heart beating in my feet instead of my chest!

They were all cosily seated in the living room when I walked in, acting as if they owned the place. Sarah and Creepy Lincoln were drinking beer. Pixie, who must be about seventeen now but still looks like a boy with long hair, and Bryony, who's about fifteen and looks very like Pixie, were staring round-eyed at the television as if they'd never seen one before. Then it struck me that they probably hadn't. They'd grown up at Ivy House with no contact with the outside world. No school (they were home educated, though most of that was doing chores, not studying), no phone, television or internet. When they stole my makeup and tried to put it on they looked like clowns. For a second (but only a second) I almost felt sorry for them, until I remembered how vile they'd been.

I ignored them, said hello to Molly and kissed her on the nose, then called her up to join me in the sanctuary of my room. I wedged a chair beneath the door handle and took Horace out of his cage so that he could sit on my shoulder and do his rat whisper while I texted Nat to tell him we had uninvited guests. Nat knew some of the Ivy House debacle, though not all of it. I hadn't told anyone except Amy and her parents about Creepy Lincoln.

Eventually I heard them all troop upstairs. Considering the spare room is quite small, they must have had to squeeze in, with at least two on the floor, and I hoped they would be very, very uncomfortable.

On Monday morning I put Horace in his cage, got dressed at the speed of light, grabbed a snack bar and my bag, and ran out of the door before anyone was up. Molly looked very surprised, and I felt guilty about not taking her out, but I just couldn't face the Ivy House crowd. I set a new record for the earliest arrival at school, ever, and found it really hard to focus all day. All I could think about was whether they'd be gone when I went home.

And guess who was still there, looking as if they'd moved in for good? Yes, you're right. Mum looked a little uncomfortable, Dom looked totally relaxed (well, he'd lived with them for years), and the Dorm Demons smirked at my horrified expression when I walked in to find them firmly ensconced on the sofa with the television blaring. Pixie had clearly staked her claim on the remote control and Bryony was wearing one of my tops.

I turned around and almost ran to Homebase for a lock and key for my bedroom door, and phoned Nat to ask him to come and put it on for me.

The very worst people from the Ivy House crowd showed all signs of having moved in with us.

CHAPTER 20

KIERAN

Back on the road. This time it was easier. There was less tension between us, partly because I tried really hard to be upbeat and cheerful, even if I didn't feel it, and partly because I hardly drank, even at the parties. That wasn't easy, but I needed to feel in control, otherwise there was a danger I'd go to pieces publicly. Plus, I didn't want to risk wrecking another gig. Although that would certainly be an easy way out of the band, it wouldn't be fair on the others.

We never see much of the areas we go to on tours, because the time is spent travelling, gigging, partying and sleeping. But something about Scotland really got to me. I loved the musical accents; harsher in some areas, softer in others, but all with a lilt that my ears easily tuned into. The hills and the heather, wild as the landscape was in parts, tugged at something deep within me.

The cities where we performed – Glasgow, Edinburgh, Inverness, Aberdeen – weren't so different to other cities, in the sense that they were full of buildings and people, but I managed to persuade Dave, our manager, to let me slope off alone early one morning to go and visit Edinburgh Castle. It was a magical sight, even from a distance, rising out of the soft light of dawn. It was too early to go up and gain entry so I took photos from below with my phone, marvelling at the craggy volcanic rock that it rested on. I thought of sending one to Lainey, and immediately decided against it. It was time I accepted the situation and found a way to make peace with myself.

The music had a new cohesion. I suspected that it was because everyone was making a huge effort to be polite to each other to stave off the usual arguments that always erupted towards the end of a tour. I also suspected that Freddie may have told the others to be more tactful around me. That was irritating, if it was true, but it made for easier relationships. We jammed together in the van as we drove to gigs, came up with some interesting riffs that sometimes developed into songs that had real potential, and did our best to clear up some of the mess of takeaway boxes and cartons.

On the drive back home, Chris moved carefully down the camper and hurled himself into the seat beside me. He drummed out a complex rhythm on his thighs with the flat of his palm, glanced sideways, and grinned.

"Good tour, eh?"

I nodded. "It was."

Freddie and Mike were squabbling amiably about whether the newest song should start with a minor chord, and Freddie quickly glanced over at me and Chris, and grinned.

"From minor to major," he sang out. "That's us, guys!"

We all laughed. For just a moment I wondered what my life would have been like now, if not for Teen Star and that song. Maybe I would have still been at school, preparing for university. I would have had more precious time with Estelle. Lainey and I would still have been together, the press would never have heard of us, and Dahlia Dean and the girls who followed after her wouldn't have been interested in me. But I'd always known we would make it at some point, so perhaps something else would have catapulted us into the limelight, anyway.

The trip home was light-hearted, all of us keen to take a short break before we started recording the new album. The others were going back to families and friends, and Chris couldn't wait to see his girlfriend, Anna. I tried not to think about the quiet house in Bath and Thomas's newly-lined face.

CHAPTER 21

LAINEY

Nat met me at Homebase so that he could help me choose the right lock. It needed to be strong, with a key, and I wanted a Yale lock but Nat said that may be taking things a little too far. After all, they surely wouldn't be staying much longer. I wasn't convinced. They looked far too settled in my home already, and past experience had taught me that they were very, very thick-skinned. I insisted and bought a Yale lock. Nat was keen to get a good look at the causes of months of misery, which unsettled me a bit. I had the impression that he was feeling curious rather than protective, but put it down to me being totally, totally freaked out by the horrible turn of events. We walked home together, hand in hand.

They all looked up when we came in, and made a big point of saying hello to Nat, who was disgustingly friendly and asked how long they were staying. Sarah just smiled and shrugged, and my heart sank even further. Dom was in the armchair, watching television with the Ivy House crowd. Sarah and Creepy Lincoln had taken over one sofa, the Dorm Demons were stretched out on the other one, and I had the strangest sensation that this wasn't my home any longer. Molly got up, wagging her tail, then lay down again.

I went into the kitchen, where Mum was cooking (I had a feeling that chickpeas were probably on the menu).

"Mum, they can't stay here! Get rid of them, please," I pleaded.

Mum put the flan she'd been making into the oven (chickpeas, mushrooms and spinach – I *knew* it!) and turned to face me.

"Lainey, I'm sorry about this. They weren't invited, and I know you had a rough time with them ...."

"*Rough*? They were horrible to me!!" I shouted. Mum quickly closed the kitchen door.

"They're only here for a few days. Please try to be polite."

"How can you do this to me? I can't stay here. I'll go to Amy's until they've left."

Mum took me by the shoulders. "No you won't, Lainey. If you do that they'll have won and it's likely they'll stay even longer. Now, I'm not thrilled about this, but we have to put up with it. It won't be for long."

I shrugged free. "You are the worst mother in the world," I told her, then rifled in the cupboard under the sink to find the tool bag and stormed back with it into the living room to get Nat. Yes, I felt a bit mean that she cried, but honestly, what would you do if your own mum refused to protect you?

Nat was sitting on the arm of the sofa, with Pixie and Bryony hanging onto every word and gazing adoringly up at him. I mean, what is it with boys? They did the same with Kieran when he visited me at Ivy House, and Nat, like Kieran, just let them. I was about to flounce upstairs when I realised that I'd be playing into their hands, so I took a deep breath, went over and kissed Nat on the cheek, took his hand and quietly led him upstairs. To my embarrassment and fury, Creepy Lincoln clapped his hands loudly, shouting "Attagirl, Lainey!" My face was scarlet by the time we got to my room.

It took a while, but Nat finally got the lock fitted. No-one would be able to get into my room without the key, and I could flick the latch on from inside and feel safe, without the need to pile furniture against the door. I let Horace out of his cage so that he could sit on my shoulder, and we sat down on my bed, side by side.

Conversation between Nat and me:

Nat: Lainey, you don't think you're being just a bit over-dramatic, do you?

Me: Absolutely not. You have no idea what they put me through!

Nat: They're trying to be friendly.

Me: With you, not with me. Didn't you notice that?

Nat: That's because you were being hostile.

Me: Whose side are you on? You're supposed to be my boyfriend!

Nat: I'm not taking sides.

Me: Well, you should be. They hate me.

Nat: They've led sheltered lives and they don't know how to act around other people.

Me (Incredulous): Are you *defending* them?

Nat (Standing up): I think I'd better go home.

I was stunned speechless. My boyfriend, my lovely Comfy Slippers boyfriend, was being totally unreasonable!

Nat left quietly and I sat on my bed, listening to Horace's rat whispers and wondering what on earth was going on. I can tell you, though, that I was very, very disappointed by Nat's attitude!

I went downstairs when Mum called me, took a plate with some flan and baked potatoes, and went up to eat it in my room.

CHAPTER 22

KIERAN

Her name is Saffie, Saffron, and she came running out, squealing, when we arrived back in London and started unloading Chris's gear outside his parents' house. She threw her arms around Chris, and he lifted her up and swung her around. Freddie, Mike and I exchanged puzzled looks as Alan, our driver, dumped another couple of bags on the ground. He'd only been talking about how he couldn't wait to see Anna, his girlfriend, as the camper van turned the corner into his road, a couple of minutes ago.

Chris caught our expressions and laughed. "Guys, it's not what you think," he said. "Meet Saffie, my cousin. She's been in Australia for two years and I had no idea she was back!" He put Saffie down and introduced us all, and she stepped forward and shook hands solemnly, though the dimples by her mouth made her look mischievous. She was small and very pretty, with hazel eyes and nut-brown wavy hair that flowed past her shoulders, and she seemed to hold my hand and gaze directly into my eyes for just a fraction longer than with Freddie and Mike.

Chris's parents stood in the doorway, waiting for the excitement to die down, then stepped forward. Harry, his dad, flung an arm around his shoulder and gave him a brief man-hug, but was soon pushed aside by Ellie, his mum, who enveloped him in her arms until he shrieked to be released. Laughing, Chris invited us in.

After cups of tea and the offer (declined) of a meal, we were ready to hit the road again to take the rest of us home. As we climbed back into the camper, Chris poked his head through the door.

"Saffie's keen to visit Bath, apparently. Would you show her round if she comes over for the day?"

I could see Saffie standing just inside the garden. If she'd looked hopeful I would have said I was too busy, but her expression was of aloof amusement and it intrigued me. I nodded and told Chris he could give her my landline number. My mobile number is shared only with the band and management, and Thomas and Lainey. As we drove off I glanced back out of the window. She stood still but raised her hand, and I nodded.

We dropped off Freddie and Mike, and finally I got home. It was a relief to carry my gear through the door, and even more so as Thomas hurried out of his study, patted me on the shoulder and said how good it was to see me, and helped me carry everything into the hallway. I slumped, exhausted, at the kitchen table, then raised my head.

"Is that cooking I can smell?"

Thomas smiled, picked up the oven gloves that Estelle had always kept on a hook on the wall, and opened the oven door with a flourish.

"I thought you'd need a home-cooked meal, so I made a roast," he told me proudly.

Now, Thomas has never been renowned for his cooking skills, and I don't think he'd put together a meal that wasn't ready-prepared in plastic since Estelle died. The food smelled wonderful, and he announced it would be ready in half an hour or so. "I wasn't sure when you'd be back," he said.

The vegetables were very much *al dente* and the chicken was … well, crispy would be the polite word, but I ate every morsel and thanked Thomas profusely. This was a major breakthrough for him, and it was good to see him smiling and joking about how he should attend cookery classes. We talked about the tour, and his new book, a novel set in South America, and how he'd got the idea from memories of a trip he and Estelle took there before I was born. It was the first time he'd mentioned her in any detail, and I listened avidly. These were people I'd never known, strangers who were in the first flush of love, and although I could tell the memories were bittersweet, it struck me how lucky they were to have loved each other so much.

Of course, that brought Lainey back into the forefront of my mind. Could we have followed in my parents' footsteps? If I hadn't been so carried away by all the glamour, would our lives have been mapped out together? Freddie's voice intruded. 'Move on. Let her go.'

CHAPTER 23

LAINEY

Before I tell you this, you have to *promise* me that you won't laugh at my expense. Believe me, from where I was standing it was *not* funny!

The Ivy House crowd were still there on Saturday. That was six whole days of misery, and I spent as much time as I could with Amy (and poor Scotty, of course, who was very nice about not getting much time alone with his beloved). When I was home I stayed in my room, away from Creepy Lincoln's googly eyes and the Dorm Demons' sly whispers. Nat had been round once in that time, had been greeted with sickening rapture by the Dorm Demons and we ended up having a row up in my room afterwards. Yes, I could see that they never met boys at Ivy House so made the most of every opportunity. But they were still being snide with me, and had taken over my home, and Nat let them flirt with him! So, Nat and I hadn't broken up, exactly, but we needed a break from each other. Our lovely easy comfy slippers relationship was more like hopping along inelegantly with stones wedged in the soles, but I hoped that once the unwelcome visitors had left we could go back to normal.

Now, if you think perhaps I'm being unreasonable, please bear in mind that they did some very cruel things to me at Ivy House. Unlike Molly, I can't 'do' unconditional love, especially to people who are nasty to me.

Anyway. Everyone went out to explore Bath on Saturday morning and Molly, Horace and I had the house to ourselves. It was sheer bliss, knowing they wouldn't be back for hours! I made toast and curled up on the sofa in my pj's with Molly, who was very happy to have me around (and in a good mood – I admit I'd been grumpy all week and dogs do sense these things). Then I had a shower.

The doorbell rang just as I was towelling myself dry. I ran to the front bedroom and opened the window, shouting down "Who is it?" The postman stepped back and waved a parcel at me, so I wrapped the towel around me and ran down to sign for it. Then the inevitable happened. As I stepped just beyond the threshold a gust of wind blasted past and the front door slammed shut. I was stuck out on the step, wearing only a towel and with my hair soaking wet, and the front door key was back in my room. I was so shocked that I grabbed the postman's arm!

"*Ohmygod*, I'm locked out!" I said.

The postman looked at me (oh, the embarrassment!). "Back door? Or any open windows downstairs?" he asked. I shook my head despairingly.

My phone, of course, was upstairs, too, so I couldn't call Amy or even Mum, and I certainly wasn't going to walk the streets of Bath to Amy's house in my towel in case I got arrested for indecent behaviour. I was mortified.

"Do you have a mobile?" I asked hopefully. I mean, everyone has mobiles now!

The postman shook his head. "Well, I do, but the battery's dead. Forgot to charge it last night," he said helpfully. And then he left me on the doorstep to carry on delivering mail!

I went next door to ask for temporary shelter, but no-one was home. The Green Park Saturday market is, unfortunately, very popular. There's no access to our back garden from the front, so there I was, stuck on the doorstep clutching a parcel, getting colder and colder as my wet hair soaked through the back of my towel. I sat down, feeling that things really couldn't get any worse.

A few people strolled past (not many, thank goodness) over the next hour, giving me strange looks as I shrank as far back against the door as possible. Then Pixie and Bryony came round the corner together, minus the adults, and burst out laughing when they saw me. I must admit, it's the first time I've ever been relieved to see them!

Perhaps now is a good time to call a truce, I thought. I smiled and waved. They smiled too, but not in a nice way, exchanging glances as Pixie put her hand in her pocket and took out the front door key. All I could think was that at last I could go inside and get dressed!

I stood up, clutching my towel tightly, and tried to squeeze in front of them as Pixie moved to fit the key in the lock. Bryony elbowed me aside as the door swung open, pushed in after Pixie, and shut the door in my face!

I shouted for them to let me in, and hammered on the door. It stayed firmly closed. I could hear the Dorm Demons laughing and Molly barking at the sound of my voice. It was another hour before Mum, Dom, Sarah and Creepy Lincoln arrived home and let me in. By then I was in tears of rage and frustration, freezing cold, and utterly mortified! Creepy Lincoln's eyes were out on stalks when he saw me, which made me feel quite sick.

Mum stood up for me for a change. She gave the Dorm Demons a good talking to in the living room. I could hear her raised voice from the safety of my bedroom – which incidentally had been raided, and two more tops had gone missing from my wardrobe. Of course I hadn't locked my bedroom door when I was in the shower, because no-one else was home. I swiftly got dressed, ran into the spare room, rifled through the bags and retrieved them. Sarah could be heard saying it was just a joke. Mum made pointed remarks about upbringing. Dom stepped in to try and calm things down. Mum shouted at Dom for the first time *ever*, and that brought me downstairs in case she needed some support.

There was quite a tableau. Mum was in the middle of the room, with The Ivy House crowd lounging on our sofas as if they didn't have a care in the world. Dom stood by the door looking upset, his loyalties clearly divided.

"Enough is enough," Mum said. "It's time for you to leave."

Then the truth came out. Tink and Aileen at Ivy House had

expelled them from the community, though they clearly weren't willing to give the reason, and they'd come to us because they had nowhere else to go. Dom tried to persuade Mum to let them stay for a few more days while they found somewhere else to stay, and in the end she agreed that they could stay one more night and had to be gone by lunchtime tomorrow. She went into the kitchen to shell chickpeas and calm down, and I followed her in and hugged her.

"Thanks, Mum," I said. She just hugged me back.

The atmosphere that day was not good. Amy was going out with Scotty, Nat said he had plans when I texted him, so I stayed up in my room, hearing the television blaring downstairs and hoping and praying that Mum wouldn't relent and let them stay. I texted Amy, who was sympathetic but distracted (I think I interrupted a romantic interlude), then I texted Kieran, who immediately offered to come round. For a moment I hesitated, then typed "Yes please!!!" before common sense could get in the way. After all, if Nat could have other plans, so could I, and I needed a friend!

The expressions on the Dorm Demons' faces when I went down to let Kieran in were so funny that it took all my willpower to not laugh out loud. Creepy Lincoln made a comment about the fickleness of youth, which I ignored, and Kieran sat in my room with me, Molly and Horace for a couple of hours. We didn't talk much. He looked really, really tired and sad, which made it even more special that he'd made the effort to come and see me. Molly gave him her best doggy kisses, which got him laughing, and we just sat quietly on the bed, side by side, watching crime drama reruns.

When Kieran got up to leave I gave him a quick hug (*not* a romantic one) and thanked him for just being there.

"When do you have to leave on tour again?" I asked. He shrugged.

"In a while," he said, then gave me one of his million-watt smiles. "We should hang out again soon. Looks as if we both need a friend at the moment."

"That would be good," I told him. And, even though I couldn't help my heart sinking a bit at the *friend* thing, I really meant it.

CHAPTER 24

KIERAN

It was beginning to feel as if Dianne was stalking me. Wherever I went, there she was, popping up like a sneakily grinning gargoyle, sidling up to me and offering to help with whatever I was doing. It was disturbing, and although I'm usually polite, I tersely brushed off her offers. Realising that she'd followed me to Lainey's after the towel debacle was the last straw. I was heading for the music shop for a quiet Saturday morning browse and there she was, sliding in beside me just as I got to Broad Street.

"Looking for something? Me perhaps?" she asked sweetly, and I shuddered.

"Yes, some privacy, so go away," I muttered. She laughed.

"Oh, I expect privacy was very much on your mind last night, then, when you went to Lainey Morgan's. It's becoming quite the *ménage a trois* with you, Lainey and Nat, isn't it?"

I stopped so fast that the woman behind bumped into me, tutted and moved around us. Dianne smirked. "Well, that caught your attention. I wonder what Nat thinks about it all?"

Anger suddenly flooded through me. Yes, Dianne had sparked it, but it was the culmination of my fury at losing Estelle, losing Lainey, my frustration with the band tours, that feeling of utter helplessness to change anything and make it better that completely took over. I turned and gripped her arm.

"If you come near me, or spread poison about me or Lainey, ever again, I'll …."

"You'll what? Hit me? Surely not. The last thing you need is bad press, Kieran dear."

"Leave me alone!" I roared.

A crowd was gathering, and I looked up to see mobile phones aimed in our direction. I let go of Dianne's arm and stalked home, seething.

It was in the papers the next morning, of course; two photos of me holding onto a smug-looking Dianne, my face suffused with rage, below a headline of *Meltdown in Dark Matter. More lovers tiffs for Kieran?* Not a pretty sight, and Alan, our PR manager, was on the phone first thing. The lecture went along the lines of "Behave yourself in public, who the hell is that girl, and is this another love affair?"

When Freddie rang and I explained, he was sympathetic.

"Look mate, it's just part of our trip. Deal with it."

There seemed to be an awful lot of things to deal with, all piling up like a multiple crash on the M4. I waited for a text from Lainey, but nothing came.

CHAPTER 25

LAINEY

The next morning the house was quiet so I got dressed and crept downstairs to make toast for breakfast, thinking I could take it back to my room and avoid everyone until the Ivy House crowd left. The squeaky door hinge alerted me just as I was buttering the toast and I turned around, hoping it was Mum. No such luck. Creepy Lincoln advanced towards me with an unpleasant gleam in his squinty little eyes. I backed away, still holding the butter knife, but he kept on coming until I was squashed between him and the wall. He grabbed my shoulders, digging in his fingers until it really hurt, and put his face about an inch away from mine so it went all blurry.

"Well, girl, you owe me a kiss," he muttered. His breath stank and I really thought I might pass out from sheer terror. I shrank back as far as I could but was pinned between him and the wall.

You've probably heard the phrase 'paralysed with fear,' but hopefully you've never experienced that awful feeling. I literally couldn't move or speak, and knew how a rat must feel when a snake's jaws are opening up in front of it, getting ready to swallow it whole. Every part of me was rigid, and then, thank goodness, some primeval survival mechanism activated.

I jabbed at Creepy Lincoln's belly with the butter knife – which, of course, was rounded, not sharp, but it took him by surprise. He yelped and grabbed my hair. My knee automatically went up, and although I was pinned too tightly to get it between his legs where it would really hurt, it made contact with his thigh. He pulled my hair so that my head was yanked painfully sideways and I screamed.

The kitchen door flew open and Mum came running in wearing her nightie, followed closely by Bryony. Mum was yelling as she tried to drag Creepy Lincoln off me but he wouldn't let go of my hair, so I was screaming too. Then suddenly I was free, and a long hank of hair was in Bryony's hand. The kitchen scissors were in her other hand.

I put my hand to my head, numb with shock, as Mum slapped Creepy Lincoln hard across the face and pulled him across the room, shouting for Dom to come and help. Bryony stood in front of me, smirking and holding up my hair like a trophy, as my legs gave way and I slid down the wall and curled up in a tight ball on the floor. Dom rushed in, took in the scene in an instant, and rushed to help Mum. A moment later Sarah and Pixie appeared in the doorway.

There was a lot of shouting. Mum wanted to call the police. She kept screaming "He attacked my daughter!" Dom was trying to calm things down, and Sarah and Bryony were yelling that it was all my fault. I just froze with my back to the wall, feeling the cold patch where my hair had been cut close to the scalp.

"Out!" Mum yelled, her face scarlet with fury. "Get out of my house right this minute and never come back!"

Dom opened his mouth and Mum rounded on him. I've never, ever seen her so angry, not even when she had to collect Dianne, Amy and me from the police station after Dianne took a lipstick from Boots Chemist. She looked seriously scary and I suddenly knew, just knew, that even though she'd been a lousy mother at Ivy House, in that moment she would have done absolutely anything to protect me. Even Creepy Lincoln looked frightened.

"Dom," she shouted, "If you even attempt to defend these dreadful people, you will be leaving with them!"

If I'd had the strength I would have applauded. Dom looked horrified and asserted that he wasn't defending them, he was just trying to calm things down.

Mum took hold of Creepy Lincoln's ear and marched him out of the house, slamming the door as soon as he was on the other side. She came back in the kitchen, took the hank of my hair out of Bryony's hand, grabbed her roughly by the arm and threw her outside, too. Molly ran downstairs and cowered beside me, shaking.

In the meantime, Sarah and Pixie went upstairs, with Dom following. A moment later they reappeared with their bags and stalked out of the house, slamming the door behind them. Mum came over to me as Dom slipped back into the kitchen, and they both lifted me up to help me onto a dining chair. Mum's face was still scarlet with anger, but she carefully put my hair on the table and then wrapped her arms around me.

Once I started crying it seemed I'd never be able to stop.

Dom put the kettle on (oh, the Englishness of that simple act!) and Mum just held my head against her shoulder and stroked my hair, murmuring. "It's okay, sweetie, it's okay". After a while I managed to catch my breath properly and the sobs tailed off. Dom made mugs of Hot Chocolate for all of us and sat in the chair beside me, patting my arm carefully.

When I could speak coherently I told then how Creepy Lincoln had followed me around at Ivy House. Mum was horrified and again talked about calling the police. Dom said it was unlikely they would pursue it, as I wasn't hurt and there was no evidence.

"Not hurt? No evidence?" Mum hissed. 'Look at her beautiful hair!'

That set me off again. I'd had long hair all my life, and now there was a huge chunk of it missing, almost to my scalp. I was devastated.

By the time we'd all had two mugs of Hot Chocolate, Mum had calmed down and Dom was looking very relieved. Mum told me to go and have a shower and get dressed, and she would take me to the hairdressers.

"Mum, it's Sunday," I said. "They'll all be closed."

"Lainey, I will find a hairdresser for you if I have to drive all the way to London," she told me, and I believed her. Seeing her in full Warrior Mode, I wouldn't have been surprised if she insisted a salon opened just for me. I went upstairs to shower and dress, trying not to look at my hair, and by the time I came down she'd Googled salons in Bath and booked me in at Essensuals, to go in immediately.

The hairdressers were so kind. I cried when the woman allocated to me ran a comb through my hair, told me that long hair was passé, and insisted that she'd give me a new look that would show off my features to perfection. Dom had elected to stay behind and walk Molly, who was traumatised by all the shouting and screaming, but Mum sat beside me the whole time, holding my hand.

As all my hair had to be cut short to accommodate the missing piece, I didn't recognise myself when I looked in the mirror afterwards. I now had a wispy pixie cut, but the hairdresser left some longer strands in front of my ears and at the back. It suited me, but it wasn't 'me.'

Mum took me out for lunch at Acorn Vegetarian Kitchen – a rare treat – and then we went clothes shopping. When we arrived home the house was spotless and my hair was nowhere to be seen. I thought Dom must have thrown it away, but later that week, when Mum said I could borrow her emerald drop earrings (a gift from Dad from the Good Old Days that she never wore after he left) I found my hair tightly coiled up in her jewellery box.

I only saw the photos of Kieran and Dianne that evening, when I checked the paper's TV guide. Kieran and Dianne? Together? Surely not! He was free to go out with anyone, but please, anyone but her!

Somehow I knew, just knew, that my life couldn't get any worse.

CHAPTER 26

KIERAN

Can life get any more crappy? I finally texted Lainey in the evening, after anxiously waiting all day to hear from her. "If you've seen it, I can explain." She didn't text back. Reporters had been camped outside my house, and I'd debated whether to try to sneak out of the back door, but finally they got bored and drifted away in ones and twos. What a relief!

Scotty phoned, wanting to know what was going on with Dianne, who'd stuck the press photos on the kitchen wall with blu-tack. It was a bit tricky, as he's her brother, so I tried not to rant too much and hoped that he would explain everything to Amy, who would then pass it on to Lainey, seeing as they're best friends. Scotty isn't Dianne's biggest fan, the poor bloke has to live with her and the hordes of kids there, so he was surprisingly okay about it and had a few choice things to say. I hoped he'd say them to her, too, and get her off my back. He mentioned she was in a relationship with John Carter, and couldn't understand why she'd be following me around. I sighed and wished John Carter all the luck in the world. He was going to need it.

The landline rang again just as I replaced the receiver. I picked it up but stayed silent, waiting in case it was a reporter.

"Hello? Hello?" The voice was young, and female. "Do I have the right number for Kieran?"

My heart sank. Someone must have passed on my number to fans. I stayed silent.

"Hellooooo. This is Saffie, Chris's cousin." I sighed with relief.

"Hi Saffie. Kieran here. Sorry, I thought you were a journalist."

She laughed. "Phew. That was beginning to weird me out. I'm coming to Bath tomorrow, just for the day. If you're free to show me around anytime, it would be great to get together."

As my day was likely to be spent trying to write songs, worrying about Lainey's lack of communication, and wondering what the hell Dianne was up to, the prospect of spending time with someone who was not only pretty but seemed fairly uncomplicated was a no-brainer. We arranged to meet at the train station (I'd be in disguise, with my woolly hat, a hoodie and dark glasses) at midday. She joked that she'd look out for a dodgy character lurking near the entrance, and rang off.

Suddenly my evening had become brighter.

CHAPTER 27

LAINEY

You know that feeling when someone has really, really upset you and you want to wake them up? Okay, let's be honest – you want them to feel as bad as you do. That's how I felt about Nat not being supportive over the Dorm Demons. I mean, for goodness sake, he was almost flirting with them! So, when he texted to ask whether I'd like some company for the evening, I was tempted to say no, then texted back to say he could come over. I didn't mention my missing hair because I kind of thought the shock would do him good. I hadn't even told Amy – she needed some time with Scotty, and I knew she'd be furious and would come rushing round with every item in her makeover kit to try and make me feel better. I couldn't bear to even look in a mirror. And I certainly didn't want to think about Kieran and Dianne canoodling and having lovers' tiffs, so I ignored his text when it came just after Nat's.

Mum and Dom were in the kitchen, drawing designs for a new piece of jewellery when Nat arrived. When I opened the door, Molly and Sam greeted each other with delight, Nat's jaw dropped almost to his chest and his voice rose at least an octave

"Lainey! What have you done to your beautiful hair?"

That did it, of course. I burst into tears again. He immediately stepped forward and put his arms around me, and I could just about hear him over my sobs. "If it's upset you so much, why did you cut it off?" he asked.

"I didn't," I wailed. And poured out what had happened.

Nat was contrite about not realising how nasty the Ivy House crowd were. He stepped back, smoothed the very short hair on top of my head, and apologised. We made Hot Chocolate and sat on one of the sofas. I was too tired to even talk much, so we watched a film, Inception, with Nat's arm tight around me all the way through. I didn't understand much of it, but it took my mind off how I must look. Molly and Sam lay on the floor in front of us, resting against each other.

I had the distinct feeling that Nat didn't like my new hairstyle. He kept looking sideways when he thought I hadn't noticed. In the end it started to bug me.

"Just say it," I told him.

"Say what?"

"That you think it looks horrible."

"It just looks different," he said, defensively. "I'll get used to it."

"*You* will get used to it?" I yelled, getting up and switching off the DVD player. "Well, hooray for you, because it's going to take *me* quite some time!"

Nat stood up and moved towards me. "Look, Lainey ...." The dogs stood up and looked expectantly at us, thinking maybe a walk was on the agenda. I backed away.

"Let's leave it," I told him. "I need some time on my own."

Nat stretched out his arms. "Look, just come here. You're taking it the wrong way. You're beautiful, Lainey, with or without your hair."

I know he was trying to be nice, but I'd had as much as I could take. I walked through the door and held it open without saying a word. Nat shrugged, clipped Sam's lead on, and walked out. Just as I was closing the door he put his hand against it.

"I'm sorry, Lainey. I didn't want to upset you. Come out with me – let's walk the dogs and calm down."

I shook my head and closed the door. Molly came over and licked my hand, and I sat down on the floor and held her close.

What the heck is wrong with boys?

CHAPTER 28

KIERAN

Saffie is fun. She's a bit of a hippy chick, all bright clothes and big smiles, eager to experience everything. We had a blast in Bath. We avoided the shops, they're much the same everywhere, and I took her to the weir and around the gardens, then we went for a trip up-river on one of the barges. The sun shone, so my dark glasses didn't gather attention (Saffie wore some too, as a joke), and no-one bothered us. It was great to just be an ordinary person, to be light-hearted and silly, and to be able to point out landmarks as we drifted over the water and to answer her questions. Not a single question was asked about the band, or fame, which was incredibly refreshing.

I really felt I'd made a friend.

Back on dry land, we sat outside The Boston Tea Party, drinking coffee and people-watching. It made a nice change to be the observer, rather than observed. Saffie made up stories about the passers-by and we laughed a lot. I didn't take her back to the house, just in case any reporters were lurking around, and when I explained this she said she understood.

"Chris doesn't seem to get the hassle you do," she mused. "Maybe it's because the lead singer always seems to get the most attention. Or maybe because he's in a steady relationship."

I shrugged. My relationship with Lainey had been given way too much attention and had been anything but steady. I was grateful that Saffie didn't mention that.

When her train back was due I walked her to the station. She hugged me and said thanks for a great day.

"We can do it again, if you like, next time I'm back," I suggested.

She smiled. "I'd like that. Or you could come to London. Not that you need showing around, I know you used to live there," she added hastily.

"That would be great," I told her, and kissed her cheek as she turned to go. She smiled and hugged me again.

"I like you," she grinned, and ran off.

Too many people have darned smartphones now. I guess it was inevitable that someone would take sneaky pictures.

CHAPTER 29

LAINEY

Ha! Dianne has competition, it seems. Kieran was in the papers again, with another girl this time, and definitely canoodling. I couldn't believe how much it hurt. I texted Amy, who still didn't know about the Hair Drama.

"Having a v v v BHD. Hot Chocolate at your place?"

Amy texted right back. "Come. Now!!"

I went.

The thing about Best Friends is that they're always truthful, and they're nearly always supportive (except when you try to pull the wool over their eyes). Amy is the best friend ever, and I don't know what I'd do without her.

She gasped when she opened the door, dragged me inside uttering *Ohmygod* over and over, and plonked me down on the sofa, sitting close and staring at me with huge blue eyes. I winced. The moment of truth had come.

"Lainey, you look *amazing*!! I never imagined you'd cut your hair, but it really, really suits you. You look like a pixie or an elf. You even have the little pointy ears!"

I burst into tears. Again. And told her how I'd gone from long-locked to shorn.

Now, Amy doesn't usually swear, but what she said really was unrepeatable. I had to cover my own ears! After cursing Creepy Lincoln and the Dorm Demons to suffer the agonies of every incurable plague under the sun (and all at the same time), she ruffled my hair.

"Actually, those bottom-dwellers did you a favour. You look stunning – like a tall, gamine model. In fact, watch out, I bet the scouts will be stopping you in the street every time you go out!"

I wiped my wet face and blew my nose very loudly. I don't know how actresses can do touching, dignified crying, with delicate sniffly nose-blows and poignant tears rolling down their cheeks that somehow don't make their eyes all red and piggy. "Do you really think it looks okay? Nat hated it."

Amy shrugged. "Nat will come around. I expect it was a shock. I hope you warned him before you saw him. No?" as I shook my head. "Well, in that case it was your own fault."

I couldn't help but laugh. "You're right, as always."

"Well, I am your wise muse and sage, you know. You really should listen to me more. Right, go and wash your face and we'll do a makeover. You need a new look now."

Twenty minutes later she let me look in the mirror. Gone was the gauche lanky girl I'd always been, and in her place was someone I didn't recognise at all. Amy had used kohl to make my eyes look bigger, piled on lots of mascara, but kept the rest of my face looking natural. I blinked. "Who is that?" I asked.

Amy smiled over my shoulder at me through the mirror. "That is the beautiful new you!" she told me. "You'll knock Nat flat next time you see him."

Of course, I had to spoil it by mentioning Kieran, Dianne and the mystery girl. Amy shook her head.

"Oh Lainey, Lainey, when will you ever learn? Put him in the past, where he belongs. You really, really need to move on." She turned me around to face her and looked very seriously into my eyes. "Understood?"

"Understood," I agreed.

If only it was that easy!

CHAPTER 30

KIERAN

On the road again, but this time it was an easier tour - just two weeks, going to Bristol, London, Birmingham and Newcastle, before we were scheduled to head to the studios to record the new album. I felt more positive about the band, and that reflected in a new level of harmony (on all levels) between us. I mostly stayed off the booze, just had the occasional drink after a gig instead of getting wasted, and I made an effort to talk to the others about ideas for songs and to test out new riffs with them when we had a few hours chilling out time. We all got on well, no major arguments barring the occasional clash of opinion that we ended up laughingly blaming on 'creative differences,' and I actually enjoyed myself.

Freddie took me aside while we drove back to London.

"Come and stay with me while we're in the studio. We'll have a blast," he said. I accepted immediately. Studio sessions are long and exhausting, repeating segments of the same song over and over until we get it all exactly right, and the thought of a couple of weeks in a lonely, sterile hotel room wasn't appealing. Freddie's been my closest friend for what seems like forever, and it would be good to have some time together. Mike, Chris and Dave, our manager, thought it was a great idea – though I suspected that Dave was thinking more along the lines of reduced costs with no hotel bills to pay.

I rang Saffie from my mobile, after just a minute's consideration. I figured she could be trusted not to post the number on the internet, even though we'd only met twice. She was delighted to hear I was in London, and we arranged to meet up and go to the Planetarium the next day.

"Why am I not surprised?" she asked, laughing. "With a name like Dark Matter I guessed you must be into cosmic stuff."

"Are you okay with the plan?" I asked, suddenly wondering whether she'd rather go out for a meal or to a club.

"More than okay. It's one of my favourite places," she told me.

The more I found out about her, the more I liked her.

Freddie and I spent the evening slouched in front of the TV with his parents, watching reruns of Big Bang Theory and eating peanuts. It was such a good feeling to be with a normal family (well, as normal as you can get when your son's on tour most of the time). It was chilled, and fun, uncomplicated and very refreshing.

Saffie met me at one-thirty pm outside the Planetarium, so we could go to the two o'clock showing. We looked up at the tiny points of light magically growing larger until they seemed to engulf us, travelling past planets as the narrator explained that what we were seeing were factories of the universe that create the material we're made of. I felt such a sense of awe, so small and insignificant and yet somehow part of it all. Saffie's hand curled around mine, and I held it tightly, glad to not be experiencing this alone.

Afterwards we went to a café and ate huge fry-ups, joking that we needed to bring ourselves back to earth, and sat there, talking, for hours without mentioning the band or fame, or how I was coping after losing Estelle. It was easy, relaxed and comfortable, and even though I didn't feel that powerful soulmate bond that I'd experienced with Lainey right from the first moment, I liked Saffie a lot.

Later, lying in bed staring at the ceiling, I reflected that maybe this was what I needed. A good friend, a sweet (and pretty) girl, who I could feel close to - but not so close that we'd burn each other.

CHAPTER 31

LAINEY

When I stumbled into the kitchen for breakfast this morning, Mum's WOD on the fridge glared out at me: *Inciting*. Mum was still in bed, so I guessed she must have put it there late last night.

Ooookaaay. What in the name of the Oxford English Dictionary was on her mind now? I took a pen from the pot on the side and wrote underneath it, 'Feeling combative?'

Sometimes Mum's WODs have a weirdly prophetic effect, and I always prefer it when they're what you might call, erm, *favourable*. I let sleepy-eyed Molly out into the garden (she's not a morning dog, and I can relate to that), set out her breakfast and then made myself tea and toast. Molly snaffled her meal, had another roam around the garden and went back to sleep on her bed. I went up to my room and gave Horace fresh food and water, though he was still asleep, too, and then slouched on the sofa and read until Molly woke up again and started giving hints about a walk. I looked at my watch. Bang on time, eight-fifteen am, when we always left to meet Nat and Sam by Victoria Park. I swear Molly can tell the time!

After Nat's less than enthusiastic response to my shorn hair, I wasn't sure that I wanted to see him – or that he'd even be there to meet us. But I clipped Molly's harness and lead on and went, anyway. Morning in the park was the highlight of her day.

I couldn't see Nat by the entrance, so I went inside, feeling hurt and angry. We wandered past the fish pond, and Molly almost pulled me in when she saw a water rat swimming under the bridge and lurched after it. I dug my heels in, could almost smell burning rubber, and held firm. Molly reached the end of her lead, realised I wasn't coming with her, and stopped dead before turning and trotting back to me, looking disappointed. I dug into the treats bag that was clipped to my jeans pocket, and rewarded her for paying attention, then unclipped her lead to avoid further possible water incidents. We walked on.

Just as I was musing about how shallow and faithless boys are, and how I never ever wanted to see one again, let alone go out with one, I heard my name being called. I looked back, and there was Sam, with Nat in hot pursuit, heading our way. Sam and Molly had a joyous reunion (they always act as it's been months since they saw each other) and Nat smiled sheepishly as he approached.

"I didn't know whether you were still speaking to me," he said. I shrugged.

"Come on, Lainey. I like your hair, really I do, it's just …."

"I know. I should have warned you. Sorry." I muttered.

"Look, it's you I'm going out with. Funny, slightly dippy Lainey, hair or no hair. Don't be mad at me."

He put his arm around me and kissed my cheek. My cheek! Why not my lips? I couldn't help feeling defensive and, yes, a bit combative. After all, he'd pandered to the Dorm Demons and refused to believe how unutterably ghastly they were! I stiffened and Nat took his arm away.

We walking in silence, side by side, pretending to be absorbed in watching Molly and Sam playing. The sun shone, the birds tweeted merrily, leaves rustled, and as we passed the carved tree trunk I couldn't help wondering about Kieran, and who the girl was that someone had snapped kissing him. Nat stopped and went back to the tree, and sat down on the damp grass. I stood, not really wanting to join him because it felt too weird after sitting there in the rain with Kieran.

Nat looked at me and patted the ground, a bit like I do when I want Molly to come and sit quietly beside me. I sat. Nat took my hand and I looked down at our entwined fingers.

"You don't want to go out with me anymore, do you?" he asked quietly.

"Yes. No. Oh, Nat, I just don't know. It's all gone wrong since the Ivy House crowd turned up, and we don't seem to gel anymore."

He looked sad. "I know things have changed, but maybe we could make it gel again."

"Things have changed too much, I think." I whispered, trying not to cry.

Nat shuffled around to face me, and lifted up my chin with his free hand. Molly and Sam, sensing that emotions were close to the surface, came up close and started licking both our faces.

"If that's what you want, then, Lainey. But I'd like us to stay friends. We can still take the dogs out, don't you think? They'd miss each other."

I nodded, and tears rolled down my face. Molly licked them away and I shifted my head so that I could look at Nat.

"I'm sorry," I sniffed. "You're a good person."

Nat smiled. "So are you." He stood up and helped me to my feet. "Shall we keep walking?"

"I think I'll stay here for a while," I told him. He kissed my cheek, called Sam to come, and walked off with his hands in his pockets. Somehow I got the feeling that he wasn't devastated, and that was a relief, but I felt terribly, terribly sad.

Molly and I sat beneath the tree for a while. *No more comfy slippers*, I thought. No more kissing, and he really was pretty good at it. No more cosy nights on the sofa, with Molly and Sam snuggled up against each other. I had a darned good cry, not caring how red my eyes were going to be afterwards. I'd lost Kieran, then Nat, and it seemed I really wasn't very good at relationships.

Mum's tarot reading suddenly popped into my head. Well, the Tower of Destruction had certainly happened, twice in fact, with the Dorm Demons and my chopped off hair, and now Nat and me no longer together. All those love cards were totally inaccurate, though. I was feeling very, very sorry for myself.

Finally I stood up and stretched, throwing my arms wide and taking deep breaths, like Mum does during her yoga exercises. To my amazement the flock of white doves who haunt the area suddenly appeared, swooped past, turned like a giant feathered wheel, and landed on my outstretched arms. I stood there with tears still rolling down my face, gazing in wonder as more and more birds landed on me, paused for a few moments, and then flew away.

CHAPTER 32

KIERAN

Two weeks in the studio are always gruelling, but it's amazing to hear the tracks come together after mixing's begun. They sounded good. The overall favourite seemed to be the one I still called 'Cacophony,' which we renamed 'Dance of the Elements' and which was to be the title track. After much discussion the others decided to include the sad, dreamy song I'd written, 'World of Sighs.' I was in two minds about it, partly because it felt very private, but somehow it provided a flip side to 'Dance of the Elements' and it made sense to put it on the album. Even Chris, who'd taken a while to trust me again after the debacle in Germany, was back to his usual friendly self, which was a relief, seeing as Saffie was his cousin.

I'd only seen Saffie once during recording, when she came to the studio at Chris's invitation and was allowed a preview of the pre-mixed version. She loved the album, but I caught her watching me closely in a way that I could only describe as assessing when she listened to 'World of Sighs.'

I found out later, when we spoke on the phone, that the paparazzi had been following her around. She didn't seem upset about it, just laughed it off, and I was torn between admiring her ability to cope and secretly wondering what was in it for her. I shrugged off my doubts, telling myself I was getting way too cynical.

Back in Bath for a week, I found Thomas had completed his novel and was looking lost and confused. He always gets like that when he's sent off a manuscript. I remember him telling me once, in happier times, that it must be like a woman gestating and giving birth, and then suddenly finding the child has grown up overnight and left home.

He was moping in his office, making notes for another book, when I arrived home, so I suggested we go out for a meal to celebrate. The expression of relief and joy on his face was like a knife in my heart. I rang the Bath Priory Hotel. It's expensive, and tables are usually booked way in advance, but when I gave my name we were immediately offered a table. There are some advantages to being famous.

We actually talked, for only the second time since Estelle died. Perhaps it was the superb food in a beautiful environment away from home, or perhaps it was just the right time – we'd both finished projects and needed to loosen up. Anyway, Thomas started off by saying how good it was for us to have a chance to actually connect, I agreed, and we kicked off from there.

I brought up Estelle's name first, just as we were finishing dessert. It was over a year since her death and we still hadn't spoken much about her. At her request she'd been cremated and her ashes scattered around an apple tree planted in her name in the Bath Natural Burial Meadow at Midford. Perhaps one day Thomas and I would go back there, but it was still too painful to contemplate.

"I miss Estelle too, you know," I told him. "It seems wrong to never mention her."

Thomas blinked. "I know you do, and I wish I could say something that would help. She was the love of my life, you know, Kieran. There was only ever her. And she was the perfect mother. She loved you so much."

We both had tears in our eyes. I reached over and touched his arm, the first time I'd actually touched him since Estelle's funeral, and he placed his hand briefly over mine.

"She was the best, wasn't she?" I said. Thomas nodded and blew his nose.

We shared stories of the funny things that Estelle had done, about how she would get her translation wrong sometimes when I was small, before her English became really fluent, and I told him about my 'pig' *faux pas* in Poland. It was good to be able to laugh together.

Afterwards, when we went home, we sat in the living room – a rare occurrence nowadays – and listened to an old Yma Sumac record that Estelle had always loved. Sumac's extraordinary voice dipped and soared, traversing octaves effortlessly, and at the end we smiled at each other, hugged, and went to our bedrooms.

I felt as if I'd received a precious gift.

CHAPTER 33

LAINEY

Nat and I had met up a couple of times, and Molly and Sam were ecstatic to see each other, but it felt a little strange making the transition from boyfriend-girlfriend to friendship. Amy was seeing Scotty most nights, but we had a couple of girly nights together. She was sad that we'd broken up, but not all that surprised. The Dorm Demons had done their work well.

Summer burst into bloom like an explosion after two weeks of rain, and I took Molly for walks, snuggled with Horace (he still slept in my bed by my feet, despite a ban on rats in bed from Mum, and he only nibbled holes in the sheet occasionally), and thought about the future.

My GCSE results came in and to everyone's amazement, especially mine, I passed all my subjects with flying colours! My surprise talent for art had (astonishingly) gained me an A, which meant I qualified to take up the offer of a place on the Level 1 Art & Design course at Bath College in the autumn! So, I had masses of free time now and I used some of it for working on my painting skills. I was discovering a love affair with oils. They're messy, they dry slowly (very, very slowly), and you can paint in layers and add all sorts of interesting things. I picked up fallen feathers and tiny stones during walks with Molly, and used these in my paintings. Somehow it felt fine to not be in a relationship. I decided that, like Marianne North, I'd never get married and would travel the world creating art that the world would remember me by. Well, we can dream, can't we?

Amy and I celebrated at Bonghi Bo's with Scotty, Hannah, Tina, Rosa, and Tina's boyfriend, Matt. Dianne wasn't invited, but of course she was there – still dribbling all over John Carter, so maybe she'd given up on Kieran. We all squeezed into a corner and had a raucous time, and I managed to ignore her. Fortunately, Dianne made no attempt to come over and stir up more trouble, and after a while I could just forget she was there and enjoy myself. It was good to see everyone.

Amy got A's for everything, of course, and was staying on to do her science A levels as part of her Grand Plan to go to university and become a scientist. We decided that we'd look for somewhere where she could study science and I could study art, and get a flat together in two years' time. It was so exciting to plan the future, especially as all I thought I was good for a year or so ago was making daisy chains!

Back home, Mum seemed to get more and more weird, with her tarot readings and yoga, and she and Dom had immersed themselves heavily in shamanism. I wasn't entirely sure what that was, but they talked a lot about spirit animals and guides, spent a lot of time playing hand drums, and I really, truly considered that I must have been a foundling. I mean, I'm nothing like my Dad, the absentee Love Rat Extraordinaire (apart from my one inadvertent venture into temporary Love Rattiness, and that was in the past). And I'm certainly not like Mum, with her WODs and her esoteric ideas, though I do admit to shelling chick peas – but I think that's just because it really is quite relaxing.

So, I determined to enjoy being single, didn't even look at boys (well, not often – I'm human, after all, and hormones can be a real pain), and wiped my mind clear every time I thought of Kieran. Well, I tried – he did keep popping into my head at very inconvenient moments. Amy said she was proud of me.

You know how you slip into a routine that feels easy and comfortable, and it seems that it can carry on forever? That's how it was for a whole month. But, of course, life never does stay on a nice even path, does it?

CHAPTER 34

KIERAN

The sun was shining and I felt more at peace than I had since Estelle's death, so I decided to go for a walk in the park. One weird thing about becoming famous is that a lot of your old friends don't feel comfortable with you anymore – unless they're band members and are going through the same thing. People think you've changed, even if it's only your lifestyle that's different. Come to think of it, I had changed a lot. I felt a lot older, more suspicious of motives, constantly having to resist the urge to look over my shoulder in case a photographer or three was lurking or following me.

I missed just being able to go and hang out with Scotty and the guys from school. Scotty was always slightly distant with me when I saw him, even though Lainey and I had sorted out our past. Some of the others were over-friendly in a way that felt false, and this was confirmed when I overhead Larry Watson boasting about how he was Kieran Kamau's buddy – as if I was a prize that could boost his own ego. So, I spent a lot of time alone when I wasn't in London or touring.

The park was shady and cool, and I slipped past the skateboarders and the children's area in my anonymous sunglasses and pulled down my skater cap, and wandered past the pond and through to a quiet area beneath the trees. My mobile rang and Harry Woods' name flashed up. I slid my finger across the screen to accept the call.

Harry's my agent. He represents all of us in the band, but so far I was the only one he stayed in touch with much - unlike Dave, our manager, who sorted all the gigs and watched us like a hawk to make sure we didn't mess up.

"Harry," I said.

"Hey Kieran. I have an offer of a role in a film for you."

I groaned inwardly. The previous part I'd had was just after Estelle died, and I was convinced that a zombie could have acted it better.

"I'm going to be touring again soon, Harry," I said, looking around to make sure no-one was close by and moving deeper into the trees. "Plus, I'm a rubbish actor."

Harry laughed. "They wouldn't be offering you the part if they thought that. Anyway, filming will be in Bath, with the first scenes around the Royal Crescent."

"So it's a period drama?" That was a no-brainer. Loads of historical dramas use the famous Royal Crescent as their backdrop, and I wondered how the residents there coped with the constant upheaval of their access being blocked and people in costume swanning around in front of their homes.

"Actually, no. It's a thriller. The potted storyline is boy meets girl, they fall in love, but girl has a secret past that catches up with her and murder and mayhem ensue."

I was intrigued. "So who's the character they want to cast me as?"

"Take a deep breath, Kieran. The romantic lead." Harry carried on breathlessly, while I stood in shocked silence. "Seriously, this is too good an opportunity to turn down. One of the starring actors will be Jack Munroe."

Now, Jack Munroe is one of my heroes. He has a huge acting range and has never made a bad film. He's won two Oscars and is already hot favourite for Supporting Actor in the Academy Awards for his part in *A Woman in Eden*. The thought of acting (and especially acting badly) beside him was terrifying.

"Bloody hell, Harry. That's way out of my league! Thanks, and all that – it's a huge compliment – but no thanks."

Harry chuckled. I heard a click and intake of breath as he lit a cigarette. "The producer doesn't think so. Six weeks filming, you wouldn't have to be there for all of it, and I've already talked to Dave and he can figure out timing with any tours that are coming up. You really should do this, Kieran. It would be a crime not to."

I could feel a panic attack coming on.

"Let me think about it and get back to you," I stuttered.

"You have twenty-four hours and not a minute more. Call me as soon as you've decided."

Harry hung up abruptly. I guessed he wasn't thrilled that I hadn't tap-danced on the spot and screamed "Yes!" After all, anyone else would bite off the hand that offered them a role alongside Jack Munroe.

I sat down on the grass, mostly because my legs suddenly felt distinctly shaky, and mulled it over. I hadn't enjoyed the last experience of filming. The timing was wrong, and besides, what no-one tells you beforehand is how much time you spend just sitting around, waiting, or repeating the same line over and over to get exactly the right timing and inflection. My passion had always been music, and I didn't want anything else taking over from that. Plus, you're even more public as an actor than as a musician, because more people watch films than go to gigs. That didn't appeal to me, either. I sat back against a tree and looked up, watching clouds lazily passing by. Tomorrow I would call Harry back and say no.

My phone rang again. I answered automatically, just as I realised, too late, it was an unknown number.

"Kieran Kamau?" The voice sounded familiar but I stayed silent, wondering if it was the press. "This is Jack Munroe. Are you free this evening? I'd like you to come over for dinner to discuss the film offer, in case you need persuading."

I was actually speechless for a few moments. Presumably sneaky Harry had passed on my number.

"Um. Well. Thank you. I'm in Bath right now. Where are you?" You know that feeling of knowing you must appear to be a total idiot. Yes, that's how I felt.

Jack Munro was smiling. I could hear it in his voice. "We're not far from you, in the Farmborough area. Text your address to this number and I'll send a car to pick you up. Will eight o'clock suit you?"

I mumbled "Yes" and added "Thank you. I'll look forward to meeting you" as an afterthought. The man must think I was a total dolt.

Getting up, dusting the grass off my butt, and pulling my hat further down, I kept my eyes focused on the ground and hot-footed it back home to get showered and ready. Nervous nowhere near expressed how I was feeling. Petrified was more like it. It's not every day you get to meet an icon.

CHAPTER 35

LAINEY

You know that creepy hairs-on-the-back-of-your-neck feeling that you're being followed? I used to get it sometimes when I was going out with Kieran, though mostly the photographers either suddenly popped up in front of me like rabbits leaping out of hats, or were so sneaky that I never even knew they were around until I saw my Bad Hair Days displayed in *Teen Dreaming*. Anyway, I kept getting this weird sensation that someone was watching me. It freaked me out. I mentioned it to Amy, who laughed and said my imagination was way too overactive, so I tried to shrug it off.

Then my Facebook page and emails were hacked and someone sent out messages to all my friends saying that I thought they were useless pieces of …. Well, you get the gist, I'm sure. I had no idea until Amy called me, swiftly followed by Rosa, to ask what was going on, because it never occurred to me to check my Facebook or email 'sent' boxes. I was mortified. Not only that, but the very worst BHD photos the press had taken, plus the photos of me looking a total wreck after me and Kieran finished were posted on an Instagram account in my name. I didn't even have Instagram!

In the end, Scotty managed to get into the accounts and remove everything and I changed my password, but it was really upsetting. He couldn't trace the hacker, though – he said there was a long line of IP addresses that the hacker had bounced through and hidden behind. He told me to put a sticker or something over my laptop webcam, in case I was being watched through that. It was seriously creepy!

At first I thought it could be Dianne, but she's not computer savvy enough. I couldn't imagine who would be so mean. Nat, of course, is brilliant at tech stuff, but I knew, just knew, that he'd never stoop to something like this. And we were still friends, though things hadn't quite settled into a relaxed state between us yet.

Amy believed my paranoia after that, and insisted I told Mum and Dom – not that they could do anything about it. She told her parents, who were very concerned. They must be so grateful to have a daughter whose life is always on an even keel!

It's not conducive to peace of mind when you're constantly looking over your shoulder. I was turning into a nervous wreck, and in the end I rang Aunt Bee, who's always sympathetic and who has lots of Creative Ideas.

Aunt Bee was worried, and nearly deafened me by shouting to Jack, forgetting to cover the mouthpiece. Jack came on the line and asked whether I'd feel more comfortable coming to stay with them while he got 'his guys,' whoever they are, to investigate. I said no, then changed my mind and said "Yes please." It would be good to have a break, at least, and Mum was never what you could call a protective parent. She and Dom hardly even clocked that I was around so certainly wouldn't notice anyone stalking me – even if a stranger walked into the living room. They were so wrapped up in each other. Gross.

I rang Amy to let her know where I was going, left a note for Mum and Dom, who were out, and packed a bag or two of essentials. Well, my entire wardrobe of summer clothes, plus all my makeup, some books, my laptop, my art stuff, and Horace in his cage do count as essentials! I took Molly, too, because I knew we'd miss each other, so another bag had to be packed with her food and grooming kit.

Aunt Bee drove down to pick me up and didn't make a single comment about it looking as if I was moving in with them. She sounded really excited about having me to stay, even though I'd wreaked havoc at their party. I wished they'd been together and living in the area when Mum made us move to Ivy House – I could have lived with them, instead! But, of course, she and Jack didn't meet until they worked on the film together and (sigh) fell deeply in love. Somehow they seemed romantic, unlike Mum and Dom. It's just too weird seeing your mother canoodling.

Their house is beautiful. It's a big farmhouse with lots of luxurious fittings. The bedroom they put me in is the size of our entire upstairs – and I have my very own bathroom attached to it. I put Horace's cage on top of a chest of drawers, unpacked my bag, hung up my clothes and put my shampoo and conditioner in the bathroom. No need for hair straighteners now, of course, because my hair's still really short. Molly was busy exploring the huge garden while I put my things away – she probably thought she was in doggy heaven! Afterwards, I went downstairs and found Aunt Bee and Jack in the kitchen, chopping a massive pile of vegetables. They told me that Jack has a guest coming for dinner to discuss a film, so I said I'd stay out of the way. I was hoping it wouldn't be anyone I'd knocked over at their party.

"Don't be daft, Lainey," Jack said. "We'll all have dinner together and then we'll have our meeting in the drawing room afterwards."

Aunt Bee positioned me on the far side of the huge farmhouse table and put a chopping board and knife in front of me. "You're on carrots and broccoli, so get chopping," she said with a grin.

I got chopping, hoping Jack's meeting wasn't with someone who'd been at That Party where I made such an idiot of myself, and not having the courage to ask him. My currently sagging self-esteem couldn't take much more of a battering.

CHAPTER 36

KIERAN

I was feeling as antsy as a lost dog by the time Jack Munroe's driver arrived to pick me up at seven-thirty pm. Should I call him Mr. Munroe, or Jack? How the hell do you try to hold a normal conversation with someone who's inspired regular bouts of awe and respect? He'd sounded friendly on the phone, but I couldn't imagine why someone with his elevated status would want me to act alongside him. It occurred to me that maybe my bad acting would make him look even better, but I instantly dismissed that. I'd heard that he was incredibly generous about not just sharing the limelight, but actually making sure his co-workers shine.

And, ultimately, why was I going to meet with him when I'd already told Harry I didn't want the part? It was curiosity, pure and simple.

We drove in silence, and I rubbed my already sweaty palms along my jeans and took some deep breaths.

Jack opened the front door when he heard the car pull up, welcomed me with a warm handshake and greeting, and led the way into a large living room with huge, squashy sofas and not an Oscar to be seen. I wondered where he kept his awards.

"Sit down," he told me, as he threw himself onto one of the sofas. I sat. "Dinner will be ready in a minute, so I just wanted us to get acquainted first."

I took a deep breath and asked what I should call him. "Jack," he said with a grin that I knew could melt women's hearts the world over. "What else? Fred? Louis?"

That made me laugh. "Well, I was wondering whether it should be Mr. Munroe."

'That would make me feel like my father. We don't stand on ceremony here, Kieran. Now, did your agent tell you the plot?"

"Just that it's boy meets girl, they fall in love, but she has a past that causes problems," I mumbled.

Jack smiled and leaped up to open a drawer. He took a folder out and handed it to me. "That's it in a nutshell, but it's a complex thriller. The current working title is *Finding Scarlett*. Basically, the girl was adopted as a baby, and it turns out that her father, who's a political fugitive, manages to trace her and spirits her away. However, her adoptive parents are being paid to watch her by those in power, who see her as a pawn who could conveniently catch him for them, so there are a lot of twists and turns. I'll be playing the father, and we want you as her boyfriend who gets caught in the middle and hasn't a clue who the good guys and the villains are. The boyfriend's a musician, so the role won't stretch you too much. Here's the script. I thought we could have dinner and get to know each other, and then just read some of it through together."

An audition? Now I was really nervous.

"Before you panic, it's not an audition. I just want you to get a feel for the character and the story. I honestly think you'll like it."

I thought of all the actor/musicians out there and asked "Why me? So many other people could play this role really well."

Jack grinned. "We want someone authentic, a real musician who can act, and you have the charisma we're looking for, Kieran." I didn't feel able to respond to that.

The door opened, and who should come in but Lainey's Aunt Bee! She looked as shocked as I felt, and said "Jack, why didn't you tell me it was Kieran coming over?"

Jack looked confused. "I didn't know you knew each other," he said. Clearly, neither of us read the papers. I had no idea they were together, which was pretty clear by the way he put his arm around her and kissed her cheek, and Jack must have missed all the drama over me and Lainey. I guessed that was over with by the time he and Bee must have got together.

Bee stretched out her arms, and I got up and hugged her. I'd always liked her.

"Well," she said, "Lainey will be surprised!"

"How is Lainey?" I asked. It seemed so long since we'd last spoken.

Bee laughed. "Oh, you can ask her yourself. Come into the dining room. Dinner's ready."

To say I was feeling confused was the understatement of the year. That gave way to total shock when I followed Jack and Bee through and there was Lainey, setting out wine glasses on the table, and Molly lurking under the table in the certain knowledge that food was about to be served. Molly leaped out and hurled herself at me, her thrashing tail knocking a glass flying. Lainey looked up and saw me, jumped and dropped another glass, fumbled to pick it up and just stood, open-mouthed.

Holy mackerel! She'd cut off her hair, and delicate tendrils framed her face and made her eyes huge. She looked like a beautiful, ethereal woodland sprite in a green floaty top and jeans. I felt my jaw drop, and made an effort to close my mouth. We both spoke at once.

"What are you doing here?"

CHAPTER 37

LAINEY

Kieran Kamau, the BOMD, appeared like a longed-for ghost from the past, and clearly hadn't expected to see me, either. All I could think was that I hadn't seen him since before the hair disaster and he must think I looked awful. He looked utterly gorgeous. He sat opposite me at the table and just stared with eyes like the proverbial saucers while Aunt Bee ladled out casserole and fetched garlic bread that was warming in the Aga. To say I felt mortified was a gross understatement - I could feel my whole face burning. Jack seemed amused.

"I gather you know each other," he said.

"Um, yes," I muttered, feeling as if my teeth were all in the wrong places. "We're .... old friends." Kieran's right eyebrow went up, like it always does when he's got something to say but decides to keep quiet.

Aunt Bee gave Jack one of her looks that clearly meant "Let's talk later," and I felt so embarrassed. Fortunately, both Aunt Bee and Jack are garrulous (Mum's WOD last month), so they chatted all through the meal, and dessert (strawberry cheesecake, I love it!), and Kieran and I sat giving each other furtive looks. Every time I caught him staring at me I quickly looked away, thinking he must be as horrified as Nat was about my lack of hair. I wanted to personally slay the Dorm Demons for what they'd done to me, and my cheeks got redder and redder, which is never an attractive look.

When the interminable meal was over, and I'd shoved most of it around my plate (except the cheesecake, I ate that), Jack noticed

Aunt Bee's silent signals (very unsubtle head-jerks) and followed her into the kitchen, leaving us alone. I looked at the crumbs on my plate.

"Lainey, you look absolutely beautiful," Kieran suddenly burst out. "What a genius idea to cut your hair!"

That did it. I broke down and sobbed, and told him what had happened, and then the added bonus (not!) of someone hacking my emails and Facebook page. Aunt Bee was on her way back into the dining room, but quickly reversed into the kitchen again. Kieran leaped up and sat beside me, putting his arms around me so that I was cocooned against him. I just couldn't help nestling in, and my already fast heartbeat raced up to about a million miles a minute. His spirally curls smelled like rosemary, and I buried my face in them, soaking his tee-shirt with tears.

He just held me for a few minutes, stroking the top of my head tenderly and murmuring "Shhh. It's okay, Lainey. It's okay." I was vaguely aware of Aunt Bee and Jack coming back in and changing their minds. They went back into the kitchen.

After a while I started to feel a bit silly. I mean, Kieran has a girlfriend, and I was getting overwhelmed by all the squishy feelings I'd tried so hard to exorcise over the past few months. I pulled away, sat up, and groped around in my jeans pocket for a tissue to blow my nose with. I wasn't looking my best, as is usual when Kieran's around.

Jack came back in again holding a tray of coffee cups, followed by Aunt Bee. He looked disconcerted (she didn't, because of course she knew Kieran was the BOMD), but he acted as if it was perfectly normal for someone to have a meltdown at the dinner table. Who knows? With actors, it probably is! Kieran stayed beside me and squeezed my hand under the table.

After that, things settled down a bit. We had coffee, then Kieran and Jack went off to the drawing room to discuss the film that Jack wanted Kieran for. It seemed like everyone wanted Kieran for some reason, and I couldn't say I blamed them. Bee and I loaded the dishwasher and sat at the kitchen table.

"Are you okay, honey?" she asked. "I had no idea Kieran was

coming, or I'd have told you."

"I know," I said.

Aunt Bee is not the most tactful person in the world, but she's very observant. She mentioned that there still seemed to be a lot of chemistry between us, so I sighed and pointed out that we're friends, and I'm still in love with him, but Kieran isn't interested in anything more.

When he left with Jack's driver, I went out to say goodbye and he gave me a huge hug. "Please keep in touch, and if you need me I'll be right there," he whispered in my ear, rubbing his cheek against my hair. "You didn't answer the last texts I sent you. I miss you. And Lainey, the Dorm Demons did you a favour – I bet that would really hack them off if they knew. You're beautiful, and don't you forget it."

CHAPTER 38

KIERAN

I rang Harry first thing in the morning and told him I'd agreed to take the part. He was irritatingly smug, saying that he knew I wouldn't be able to resist Jack Munroe. My main worry was the band, but Harry had taken it for granted that I'd accept the role and had already discussed it with Dave, the manager, who'd said he would set up our gigs and recording sessions around the filming in a few months' time.

What I didn't expect was the band's reaction when I arrived in London for a series of gigs around the Republic of Ireland. Freddie was delighted and banged me on the back so hard that I had a coughing fit. He saw it as great promotion for Dark Matter. Mike didn't say much, but I could tell he wasn't exactly over the moon. Chris, however, was … well, angry is putting it mildly. He ranted about my lack of commitment and questioned whether I'd bother staying in the band if I was going to be "a hot-shot movie star," as he put it. He practically spat the words at me, and refused to listen when I told him it could only be good for all of us. Heck, I wasn't keen on even more fame, but I liked the part, I could play my guitar as part of it, and what sane person would pass up the chance to work with Jack Munroe? I didn't mention seeing Lainey because I didn't want a lecture from Freddie.

After Chris stormed off, dark hair flying, Freddie quietly muttered, "Jealousy is a terrible thing. Go for it with the film, Kieran."

Saffie, though, was thrilled and excited when she came over to

Freddie's parents' house to see me. "You'll be brilliant," she told me, her hazel eyes glowing. "And wow, I'll have a movie star boyfriend! Ignore Chris, it's just sour grapes."

That made me uncomfortable. I mean, I liked her a lot, but I didn't want to get serious, and she seemed to be looking at the long-term when we weren't even officially boyfriend and girlfriend. Plus, it really wouldn't be a good idea to get too involved with a relative of a band member – especially one who was feeling hostile towards me already. I just shrugged it off and changed the subject, feeling a bit weird that she spent all evening holding onto my arm as if she thought I might escape.

It was a relief to get on the plane to Dublin and let the roadies drive over with our van and all the gear.

If you've ever performed in public, you'll know how vital it is that everyone gets on. You're in a cramped environment with a bunch of guys who have good and bad moods, plus everyone gets cranky when they're tired, but it's great to celebrate together and feel a sense of achievement when things go well. Not much celebrating happened on this tour.

To set Chris off even more, it was just unfortunate that I seemed to have a spectacular fan base in Ireland. Girls were screaming and holding up banners that read "I love Kieran" and "Kieran for ever." Freddie and Mike, who'd got over his brief sulk, laughed it off. Dave was continually rubbing his hands together with glee as record sales hit the roof. Chris glowered into his drums and broke an unprecedented number of drumsticks, and the atmosphere off stage was tense. Nothing I said made it easier. Then Saffie turned up in Cork and hitched a ride with us to Galway, and all hell broke loose.

CHAPTER 39

LAINEY

Ten reasons to pull myself together:

1   Yes, I'm still in love with Kieran Kamau. He's still the
     BOMD. But he has Moved On.
2   Kieran is just being nice to me because he's a good
     person (other than the Love Rat experience, which is in
     the past now).
3   Kieran has a girlfriend.
4   I've got used to being unattached. Well, I thought so,
     until Kieran appeared again.
5   He thinks I'm beautiful, even with short hair. And even
     though he's just being a friend.
6   That should make me feel better about myself,
     anyway.
7   I feel rubbish because I'll never, ever love anyone like
     I love Kieran. But this will pass.
8   I will not expire from unrequited love.
9   I'm sixteen and have lots of exciting things ahead of
     me. Just because I can't get excited about them at the
     moment doesn't mean I won't be tomorrow, or next
     year.
10   It's not fetching to wallow in self-pitying misery.

Ten reasons to be grateful:

1   Kieran said I look beautiful.
2   I have Molly and Horace to whisper my deepest secrets to, and they always listen and never tell.
3   Aunt Bee and Jack are being really, really kind to me (and not canoodling in front of me).
4   Amy is still my best friend (though she'd be very, very annoyed if she realised I still Have Feelings for Kieran).
5   I'm going to college in the autumn, after a lifetime of being told I was Not Fulfilling My Potential.
6   I have my health (that's what Aunt Carol would say).
7   Actually, I can't think of anything else. I don't feel very grateful at the moment.

I curled up on my bed (where Mollie was taking up most of the space) with Horace doing his Rat Whisper in my ear while he snuggled into the top of my shoulder and fell asleep, and I imagined the future. I could just see myself as a Miss Haversham character, surrounded by dust and cobwebs and mementos of the past, growing old and wrinkly and all bitter and twisted as I contemplated what might have been.

A thought made me sit up so fast that Horace slid down my shoulder and dropped into the convenient hollow provided by Molly's front armpit (or should that be pawpit?), where he promptly went back to sleep again. It's lucky that Molly is a very tolerant hound. I was shocked at myself. I loathe and abhor cobwebs because spiders live in them! No, Miss Haversham was out. Instead, I'd be a hugely successful artist, living in a pristine house (cleaned by someone else, of course) somewhere in the Mediterranean.

My plans for the future made, I lay back down again with the best furry friends in the world, and dozed off. When I woke up a while later, Molly was lying across me, practically crushing me, Horace had sneaked down to the bottom of the bed and there was a tell-tale nibble-hole in the coverlet.

CHAPTER 40

KIERAN

Okay. Just imagine that you're spending hours every day in a van with three fellow band members, plus a roadie driver, and a girl who is convinced that she's the love of your life and has suddenly become somewhat clingy, even though you've only met a few times. Oh, and the cousin of said girl, who is also in the van, hates your guts at the moment and glares every time you speak.

Then multiply that by seven, for another week of gigs, and (just for fun) include a little addendum in which the girl (to your surprise) has a minor tantrum after each gig because other girls were trying to get you to autograph their arms, upper chests, and (in one case) a thigh. By day three after Saffie joined us I was starting to lose the will to live.

Fortunately for me, when she was in a sulk she turned to her laptop for consolation. I frequently fell asleep to the rapid tapping of fingernails on keyboard. Once, when I leaned over to ask whether she was writing a book, she slammed the top closed before I could read anything on the screen, and said it was private. It was a relief to go to our hotel rooms after the gigs, especially when Saffie was having a hissy fit over some girl.

It was Dave, who always keeps a keen eye on social media, who quietly mentioned to me that Saffie had been very busy on her laptop, tweeting about her adventures on tour with her boyfriend and Dark Matter, and had accrued a lot of followers. That explained why she wasn't upset about the paparazzi – she was actively encouraging them. I did not have a good feeling about this, and spent way too much time trying to figure out how I could extricate myself with minimum damage on all sides.

I have to admit, it was so exhausting and stressful that I just wanted to get the tour over and not have to see her again. Chris was still breaking drumsticks at such a rate that the manufacturers would surely run out by the time we returned to England, and he argued endlessly over the set list, even though we'd arranged it before we left home.

The final gig, in Tralee, County Kerry, was heaving with the press as well as the audience. I had a horrible feeling that something was going to go terribly wrong, but the gig went really well. It was afterwards that everything went haywire.

The organisers had arranged an after-gig party as a big farewell 'do.' I really wanted to leap on the first plane out of Kerry airport, but Freddie was in high spirits so I hung out with him. As usual, we were surrounded by girls wanting autographs (and sometimes more), and one girl looked a bit like Lainey. She had short, red-brown hair and huge green eyes, but was more (shall we say) buxom. She edged in between me and Freddie, and asked Freddie to sign her arm, handing him her pen. Freddie signed and had a laugh with her. Then she turned to me and shyly asked me to sign between her shoulder blades, moving in front so that I could do it. I took the pen from Freddie, started to sign my name, and suddenly the girl fell against me with all the power of a missile.

Winded, I went down like a stone, with the girl sprawled on top of me. And, on top of her, fists flying, was Saffie. Jesus! She was yelling that I clearly still preferred Lainey to her (what? She'd never mentioned Lainey before!), the poor girl she'd attacked was screaming, and it took Freddie and two security guys to pull Saffie off and march her away. Still gasping, I dragged myself upright and helped her to her feet. Blood was flowing from her nose and someone leaped forward with a handkerchief.

"I'm so, so sorry," I kept saying. She hunched against me, bleeding and sobbing. A crowd had gathered tightly around us and cameras, of course, were flashing. "Can someone get her to a hospital," I yelled. "I think her nose may be broken!"

A guy pushed through the crowd. "She's my sister," he said. "What the hell did you do to her?"

He didn't wait for me to answer. I woke up in a hospital bed with the headache from hell and, apparently, concussion where he'd pushed me and I fell against the bar and went out cold.

CHAPTER 41

LAINEY

After my Facebook account was hacked again three times in a week, I closed my account (or as closed as Facebook will let you – they never totally delete it), changed my email password yet again, and hoped and prayed that the hacker wouldn't carry on sending out venom to my friends. I'd been debating whether to text Kieran to tell him, in case he got any weird messages, but when he came to see Jack he'd mentioned he was going on tour, so I didn't want to bother him. He uses a fake name on Facebook (I'd better not say what it is) and only has a very small group of friends there, so I thought he'd let me know if there was a problem. None of the previous messages had been sent to him, it was friends I messaged a lot who were targeted.

It was Jack who told me that Kieran was in hospital in County Kerry. He and Aunt Bee had just come home, and I was pouring coffee for them when he told me to sit down because he had bad news. I immediately panicked when I read the piece he showed me in the paper. There it was, horribly dramatic, with photos of his esteemed girlfriend punching some poor girl's lights out, and more photos of Kieran unconscious on the floor, then on a stretcher.

Jack was incredibly kind. He offered to fly me over to Ireland (for goodness sake, he can even fly a plane, and has an old Cherokee Warrior that he's immensely proud of), but I politely declined – though I did throw my arms around him and tell him how unutterably wonderful he is. He seemed pleased about that, and said "It's least I can do. We're family."

I guessed we were, in a way. It was only when Aunt Bee sat beside me and enveloped me in a big hug that I noticed she was wearing a huge emerald ring on the third finger of her left hand. I grabbed her hand and held it up.

"What's this? Have you got engaged?" I asked. They both beamed.

"Yes, this morning," they said in unison.

"*OhmyGod!* That's amazing!" I threw my arms around both of them and we had a massive group hug. I couldn't think of two people who were more perfect for each other, and they both beamed and said that of course I was going to be their bridesmaid.

Talking about their wedding plans took my mind off Kieran for a while. They'd decided to just go for it, no waiting, and were planning a quiet ceremony at Bath Guildhall in a month's time, on the twenty-first of August, with just family and close friends. Apparently you have to give twenty-eight days' notice, so that was their earliest available date.

I could hardly believe it! My lovely aunt, one of my very favourite people in the whole world, was getting married. And I would be a bridesmaid for the first time ever! They swore me to secrecy because they didn't want a big press hullabaloo, which I could totally understand. I swore on my life, and on Horace's and Molly's, that I wouldn't breathe a word to anyone (except Horace and Molly).

Of course, the conversation slipped back to Kieran. How could it not, with those awful photos of him in front of us. Jack promised that he'd find out how he was, and went off to phone his agent, who phoned Kieran's agent, who rang Jack back a while later while we were drinking Hot Chocolate (well, I was, they had coffee), and making wedding plans, and I was trying not to think about Kieran lying there, brain damaged, never to recover – you know how your mind leaps instantly to the worst possible scenario!

After a few minutes he came through and ruffled the top of my head. "Kieran's awake. He has a headache, but there's no serious damage and he'll be flown home in a couple of days. I asked Harry to pass on our love."

I flopped back and sighed with relief.

That evening, Aunt Bee and Jack were out having dinner with friends (I didn't want to go, though they invited me), and I was sitting drawing designs for my bridesmaid's dress and trying not to think about Kieran, when my mobile rang. The screen just showed "International number", which usually means cold calls from companies wanting you to take someone to court for an accident you never even had. I answered and waited for the usual creepy automated voice.

It was Kieran, phoning from the hospital!

CHAPTER 42

KIERAN

Well, I'd had about as much drama as anyone can take during the past fortnight, and being stuck in hospital having brain scans wasn't something I would ever have chosen. Freddie, Mike and Dave, our manager, visited. They told me that the police had wanted to charge Saffie, but that the poor girl she'd attacked refused to press charges, which was very forgiving of her. Dave had got the girl's address and sent her flowers and copies of all our albums.

Saffie had been put on a plane back to England and Chris had gone with her.

"Look, Kieran, this isn't the right time, but when you've recovered we need to talk about the future of the band," Dave said.

My heart skipped a beat. "I'd rather do it now. Are we breaking up?"

"God, no," Dave said. He looked across at Freddie and Mike, who nodded. "We've all had it with Chris's jealousy and temper, and the lads have mentioned it to me a few times. We're letting him go. No way will it work now, especially with all this craziness from his cousin."

"Letting him go. You mean you're kicking him out?"

Dave nodded. "Already done it. He'll try and sue, no doubt, but really there's no case."

I took a deep breath and rubbed my aching head. "Oh, crap," I muttered. I felt bad for Chris, I really did. He's a darned good drummer, and we'd been friends for a long time – I hated endings. But a part of me felt relieved not to have to be in that tense atmosphere any more.

"We'll start auditioning as soon as you're home in a couple of days, if you feel up to it. We need your input, Kieran," Dave said. "I'm just sorry things have gone so sour. Still," he smiled, 'There'll be no shortage of applicants for his place."

They left soon afterwards, each of them patting me gently on the shoulder, and I lay there wondering how everything could have gone so wrong.

That evening I checked my phone. There were loads of caring messages, plus several really nasty ones from Saffie and Chris which I immediately deleted. I rarely go on Facebook but I logged in and found a string of messages from Lainey. Thinking she was concerned, and feeling touched that she still cared about me, I opened the message thread and gasped.

It was a long rant about what a crap human being I am, what a rubbish boyfriend I was, and how she never, ever wanted to have anything to do with me again. My blood ran cold and my heart pounded as I read them. Then, masochistically, I read them again. Something seemed weird. However mad Lainey must have been when she wrote them (and she'd never sent me nasty texts or emails even after we broke up), they somehow didn't sound like her. She never said "crap," for one thing, and it was repeated over and over again throughout the messages.

Then I thought about the phone message that Harry had passed on to me earlier from Jack, saying they all sent their love, and I thought I knew what was going on.

I rang Lainey from the phone by my bed.

CHAPTER 43

LAINEY

It was so great to hear Kieran's voice! He sounded tired, but said he was fine and looking forward to coming home. I almost told him about Aunt Bee and Jack getting married, then remembered just in time that I was sworn to secrecy. Instead, I said how great it is that he and Jack will be working together. He agreed, then there was a moment's awkward silence.

"Lainey, you know you told me about being hacked?"

I nodded, then remembered he couldn't see me. "Yes. It happened again this week, and I've had enough. I closed my Facebook account."

"I hate to tell you this, but it seems to have been reactivated. I've had a stream of nasty messages about how much you hate me, and there are some pretty vicious posts on your page, supposedly by you."

OhmyGod. I felt terrible! I actually wanted to curl up into a little Horace-sized ball and then disappear. Instead, I started to cry – so embarrassing. He must get sick of me bleating!

"I'm so, so sorry, Kieran. I don't know what to do!"

"Lainey, it'll be okay. Don't cry. I'm going to contact Facebook about it and try to get this sorted out. Do you have any idea who it could be?"

I ruled out Nat. He has the skills, but he's too nice to do something so mean. Scotty's on a par with Nat, but ditto to being nice. We're friends – and, even though he's Dianne's brother, if he slipped off the straight and narrow Amy would never speak to him again. Dianne isn't techie enough, though it was possible that she'd enlisted help from someone – the hatred in the messages certainly was Dianne's style, but she seemed to have gone quiet lately. What seemed most weird was that Kieran hadn't been affected before, but had been now. Maybe the hacker had only just found out Kieran's fake identity.

We puzzled over it for a while, and couldn't figure out who, or why. Kieran was sounding even more tired, so I told him to get some rest.

"Okay," he said. "Look, why don't you ask Scotty to go into the account and see what he can find out." Eurgh! The thought of sweet, caring Scotty reading the horrible stuff from my impersonator made my stomach churn. In the end, though, I agreed.

We said goodnight and Kieran promised to come over as soon as he arrived back in Bath. As I went to hang up I could have sworn I heard him whisper "Love you, Lainey." I put the phone back to my ear at the speed of light, but he was gone.

Imagination can play strange tricks. Still, I hugged myself tightly and made a wish.

CHAPTER 44

KIERAN

It was such a relief to get home. I still felt a bit wobbly, but the headache was easing and the doctors had promised me that I'd feel fine in a week or so, providing I took it easy. Dave suggested that they start the drummer auditions without me, video them all and put together a shortlist, so that I could be in on the final decision-making. That made sense.

Thomas was delighted to see me. I'd refused to let him fly over – it seemed pointless when I'd be back so soon – but he kept saying how worried he'd been. He cooked lasagne (well, it was ready-made but he put it in the oven instead of the microwave), we discussed what had happened, and he softly suggested I put it down to life's rich (and not always pretty) tapestry and to put it all behind me. The old closeness was starting to come back between us, and that made me happy.

I told him about Lainey's problems, and he sighed then looked me straight in the eye.

"You're still in love with her, aren't you?"

I nodded. "There's no-one else like her, Thomas. She's special. But Freddie said I should leave the past in the past and just be friends. I doubt she has the same feelings. I treated her really badly."

Thomas smiled and shrugged. "She's a lovely girl, and she seems to have forgiven you. The only way you'll know for sure is if you talk to her. The worst that can happen is that she'll say she just wants to stay friends, but at least then you'll know."

It was like having a light switched on in a dark room.

"Thomas, I told her I'd go over this evening. If I text her now, would you mind giving me a lift?"

He agreed immediately.

On the way, we discussed the plans he was making for another novel. He seemed excited about it, and excitement of the good kind has been in short supply since Estelle died. I felt glad for him.

A car seemed to be following us and I inwardly cursed the press, but it carried on after we turned into the driveway so I chastised myself for getting paranoid. We pulled up outside the farmhouse and Thomas turned and put his hand on my shoulder. "Just be honest, Kieran," he said. I felt a surge of love for him and leaned forward to give him a hug.

"Thanks Dad," I said. Thomas looked astounded. I hadn't called him Dad since I was ten years old. I ran to the door and rang the bell.

CHAPTER 45

LAINEY

Jack looked up and grinned as I ran past him to open the door, closely followed by Molly. He and Aunt Bee were in the living room, discussing one of the sub-plots in *Finding Scarlett* and arguing in a friendly way about whether it needed beefing up. Jack had told me the story and I thought it was great. Kieran would be brilliant as the musician boyfriend, but I knew that a lot of actors (like Jack and Aunt Bee) fell in love in real life with their big screen 'love interest,' so I hoped that wasn't going to happen again with whoever would be the female lead.

Kieran enveloped me in a huge hug as soon as I opened the door, and Molly leaped around, whining with joy. I melted into his arms, wishing I could stay there forever. He nuzzled the short hair on top of my head with his chin.

"How's my pixie tonight?" he asked.

Did he call me his?? I felt a resurgence of that old, infuriating awkwardness that had reared its mortifying head the very first time we met, and just stammered "Okay." Kieran stepped back. Behind him, Thomas turned the car around and started to drive away. I waved, and he waved back out of the window.

We went into the kitchen, with Molly in tow, and I poured orange juice for both of us and added ice cubes while Kieran crouched down and let Molly leap all over him and lick his face. I have to admit that I would have liked to do the same. Jack put his head around the door and told us to use the living room, as he and Aunt Bee were doing some script run-throughs in the library. Yes, they have a library – what heaven! So, we sat at opposite ends of one of the huge sofas and just looked at each other. Molly flopped on the rug in front of us.

Kieran looked tired, he had dark rings under his eyes, but he was still the most beautiful boy in the world. I wanted to disappear into those soft brown eyes, and actually thought it might happen if I looked at him for much longer. He leaned forward and took my hand.

"Lainey, I have something to tell you. Please would you just hear me out and then tell me what you think. I'm feeling really nervous."

'*OhmyGod*' I thought, 'He's back with that awful Saffie!' My heart sank to somewhere near the region of the South Pole, but I nodded.

"Okay, here goes," Kieran said, and took a deep breath. He looked terrified. Did he think I was going to hit him? I could feel my eyes welling up (again – so infuriating!) and I blinked hard and steeled myself to be brave.

"Fire!" Jack yelled, just as the fire alarm went off. The din was terrible, and we leaped off the sofa and ran to fling open the front door, with Molly dancing around as if she thought it was a game.

"Where?" I shouted, as Jack and Aunt Bee joined us and pushed us outside. "*OhmyGod*, Horace! He's upstairs – I have to get him!"

Jack refused to let me past. "It's in the drawing room. Stay there, I'll get the fire extinguisher while Bee phones the fire brigade." He pushed his mobile into Aunt Bee's hand as he turned back indoors. "I don't know how bad it is, I just saw the curtains were alight when I came out of the library."

Horace, my beautiful little Horace! I tried to run back inside, but Kieran grabbed me. "Stay here with Molly and Bee," he yelled over the fire alarm, and he ran inside and up the stairs. Smoke was billowing out and filling the hallway. There was no sign of Jack, and Aunt Bee was hysterical, trying to go inside. I held her back, even though I wanted to just run in with her. The smoke was getting thicker and I coughed, holding Molly's collar to make sure she didn't go in.

It suddenly struck me that Kieran didn't know where my bedroom was. He could be trapped up there. I handed Molly to Aunt Bee and ran inside just as Jack came out. He grabbed my arm. 'It's okay. I've put it out and shut the door. It caught the curtains and was just spreading to the rug under the window. Stay here until the fire engines arrive.'

"Kieran's upstairs," I cried, pulled my arm free and ran upstairs. He met me partway, with Horace in his cage and I sobbed with relief as we ran down and outside together.

A few minutes later the fire engines came racing up the drive. Jack went over and told them he thought it was safe now, and they insisted we stay in the garden while they checked. Kieran put Horace's cage gently on the ground and put his arms around Aunt Bee's shoulder and mine. We stood and watched as the men went in.

It was quite a while before they left, and Jack had a long conversation with them, looking increasingly concerned, after they came out of the house. We went into the kitchen and Jack called the police and made tea while we waited for them to arrive to interview all of us. His phone kept ringing. His agent, his manager, his parents all wanted to call in security men to be bodyguards, but he refused.

The fire wasn't an accident. Someone had poured petrol through the open window, soaking the curtains and setting them alight. The horror of what could have happened if Jack hadn't gone to get a drink shocked all of us into silence. After the police left we sat quietly, wondering who it was who hated us so much and not coming up with a single answer.

Jack insisted on booking rooms in a hotel for him, Aunt Bee and me, and on taking Kieran home. Kieran had another idea.

"Come and stay the night at my place. We have plenty of space and Thomas won't mind at all." Jack and Aunt Bee looked at each other, and gratefully agreed.

CHAPTER 46

KIERAN

Wow, that was scary. I wondered whether Lainey's hacker had started the fire. I racked my brains, trying to get a mental image of the car that had been behind us. A Mini, that was it. A dark blue, maybe black, Mini. All I could remember of the driver from looking in the mirror was that he was wearing a hat, so it was impossible to get a glimpse of his face. So, was I the target? Or was it Lainey, Jack or Bee? Who the hell would put so many lives in danger? And if Lainey was the person they were after, did that mean the arsonist had known I was going to see her and had used me to find out where she was? The thought made me feel sick.

Thomas was delighted to have guests for the night, but deeply worried when we told him what had happened. He insisted that Lainey phoned her mother to let her know where she was, even though Lainey protested. Ellen, Lainey's mum, offered to come over - which, from the expression on Lainey's face, was not what she'd expected. She said there was no need, but promised to phone the next day.

By then we were all exhausted. Somehow it didn't seem the right time to take Lainey aside and declare my feelings for her. She'd looked nervous when I'd said I wanted to talk to her, and I wondered whether she knew what I was going to say and was going to let me down gently. If so, it was no less than I deserved, but a few times I'd been sure I'd seen something in her eyes that mirrored how I felt.

It was a sleepless night. Thoughts tumbled around like Horace in his exercise wheel, and none of them brought any answers.

Jack and Thomas were deep in discussion in the study when I came down early in the morning, and Molly was stretched out at Thomas's feet. I assumed they must be talking about the fire, but then I heard them laughing together. It was such a gift to hear Thomas's deep belly laugh. I hesitated by the door, not wanting to disturb them, but Thomas saw me and called me in.

"Did you know that it was Jack's production company who bought the film rights to *The Tree of Never-Ending Delights* over three years ago?" he asked delightedly. I hadn't even known that Jack owned a production company, though I remembered a celebratory meal with Estelle and Thomas at The Olive Tree restaurant back then. The film hadn't been made, as so often happens when movie options are sold, but the synchronicity of all of us being together, years later, appealed to me.

"We've just been waiting for the finance to come together," Jack said, his eyes twinkling. "It's going to happen, sooner or later." The book won a prize when it came out, partly because Thomas is a brilliant writer, and partly because the story was so unusual. The narrator was an oak tree, and the story it told followed the fortunes (and misfortunes) of six generations of the family who owned the land where the tree had been planted. I'd read the manuscript before Thomas sent it to his publisher, and found myself enchanted by how the tree's dry wisdom and acceptance provided a foil to the human dramas as they unfolded. I couldn't imagine how it could translate well to the big screen, though Thomas had said at the time that all that was needed was a good narrator.

Bee appeared in the doorway, with Lainey behind her, and I suggested I made breakfast for everyone. A chorus of voices offered help, and Bee and Lainey followed me through. Soon we were all sitting around the table, eating scrambled eggs and toast and avoiding talking about the arsonist. It struck me that these were our first staying guests since Estelle died.

Afterwards, Jack took a call from his manager, who'd hired a private investigator, and Lainey and I made more tea and took ours out into the garden. We sat on the grass beneath the willow tree in the furthest corner and watched the sun filter down through the delicate fronds. It felt peaceful, a respite after last night's drama. I looked across at Lainey and caught her looking at me. The sun cast glints of red-gold off her hair, and I wanted to reach out and touch her.

I took a deep breath and stretched out my hand to take hers.

"Lainey Lainey, beautiful Lainey, I love you. Please will you give us another chance?"

CHAPTER 47

LAINEY

OhmyGod. Kieran still loves me. The BOMD wants us to get back together! For a moment I was speechless with shock. It was the last thing I'd expected to hear, and I felt a wave of joy roll up from my toes to my head and explode in a burst of light. I stared at him. He looked … well, scared, as if he expected me to say no.

"Yes," I said. "Yes, yes, *yes!*"

And then he kissed me, and it was the best, most wonderful feeling in the whole wide world.

We lay back on the grass for ages, with our arms around each other, kissing. I didn't care what anyone thought anymore, not even Amy (who was sure to disapprove). I forgot about the hacker, and the arsonist, and I didn't even think about paparazzi, BHDs or how I was going to explain this to anyone. Kieran Kamau loves me and I love him. That was all I could think about. And pretty soon, thinking became superfluous.

I really don't think I'd ever felt so happy in my entire life. Well, perhaps when Kieran first asked me out, nearly 18 months ago. But we were older now, and wiser. We had Life Experiences. And that old betrayal and the pain it had caused just floated away like dust in a breeze.

We may well have stayed out there forever, but Aunt Bee came out and coughed discreetly to interrupt us. We hastily sat up and dusted grass off ourselves. Aunt Bee looked delighted.

"Well, am I right in guessing you two are an item again?" she asked. We both nodded. "Well, thank goodness for that! I've been wondering how long it would take you. Sorry to interrupt, but the police are here and want to talk to you again."

Nothing, but nothing, was going to upset me now. Kieran stood up and held out his hand to pull me to my feet. For a moment we stood close, leaning into each other, and then we followed Aunt Bee back into the house.

The living room is big, but it was pretty crowded. Thomas (with Molly practically sitting on his lap – she'd taken quite a shine to him), Jack, Aunt Bee, me and Kieran, two police officers (one male, one female) and (surprise surprise) Mum, Dom and Amy took over the sofas and armchairs. I'd texted Amy last night and she'd wanted to come over immediately, but by then I was too tired to talk any more. It turned out that she'd phoned Mum, who'd offered her a lift over with them.

Amy is perceptive. She looked at me, looked at Kieran, and instantly knew we were back together. The fact that we were holding hands was probably a major clue, mind you. I waited for Judgement to come, but instead she ran over and hugged both of us.

"I'm so glad you're safe," she cried. "I was frantic when I got your text!" She looked hard at Kieran. "You'd better take good care of her this time, or you'll have me to answer to," she growled.

Kieran blushed. "I promise, Amy. Lainey means the world to me."

Amy looked fierce, but then she smiled and hugged Kieran. "For goodness' sake. I'm glad you've grown up and seen the light at last!" Kieran hugged her back, looking immensely relieved.

The police went through everything with us again, starting with Kieran noticing Thomas's car was being followed and giving a description, and then the fire at the farmhouse. Unfortunately there are no close neighbours so there were no witnesses. The police had an alert out and were checking traffic cameras in the area to try and get a number plate, so it seemed to be a matter of waiting it out until they had some information. They surmised that it was an amateur job and asked whether Kieran had any enemies. He mentioned the texts from Saffie and Chris, and they took his phone with them. He then told them about my hacker, so they said they'd get his

Facebook messages checked, too, and they took my laptop to go through. I hoped they wouldn't read my private journal, then realised that the hacker probably had and felt sick with embarrassment.

Jack's manager had arranged for the damage in the farmhouse to be repaired. Fortunately it was just the curtains and a rug, and the walls needed to be decorated throughout because of the smoke. Thomas offered to have us all to stay in the meantime, and he looked so crushed when Jack said he couldn't possibly put him to any more trouble that Jack changed his mind and thanked him profusely.

Finally Mum and Dom left, after being reassured about a thousand times that we were all fine. Amy stayed for a bit longer and then said she'd promised to meet Scotty by the weir. She invited us to join them, and Kieran and I looked at each other. Thomas quickly said that Molly could stay with him, and she looked perfectly happy so we agreed.

Our renewed relationship was going to be public knowledge very soon, anyway. We may as well get it over with.

CHAPTER 48

KIERAN

It's a strange and very uncomfortable feeling when people who were previously friends go all chilly on you, like Scotty did. I could understand why he was initially angry with me, but not why he stayed mad. Amy had reacted better than I expected about me and Lainey getting back together – I could see the relief on Lainey's face when Amy hugged me, and it matched how I felt. It's tough when best friends don't like the boyfriend. I just hoped Scotty would be okay. The altercation with Dianne that the press made such a meal of wouldn't have endeared me to him any further, for sure. So, it was with a sense of trepidation that I climbed out of Lainey's mum's car. It was tempting to cry off and whisk Lainey away somewhere else. We'd only just renewed our relationship, and we needed some time alone.

I took Lainey's hand as we followed Amy down to the weir, and had just bent down to suggest we sloped off on our own when Amy called Scotty's name and waved dramatically. I looked up and saw, too late, that Scotty was accompanied by Nat and Rosa, Lainey's friend who she's always envied because Rosa's inherited her striking Italian looks from her parents. My heart plummeted. Great. Two ex-boyfriends, (one now no longer an ex), plus a hostile former friend, and another ex-friend whose feelings towards me were currently undetermined. It was starting to look like quite a party - one that I really wished I hadn't been invited to. I took a deep breath and kept on walking towards them.

Scotty looked surprised, but said hello in a warmer tone than the last time I'd seen him. Nat, to my amazement, leaned over and clapped me on the shoulder. "About time," he said. "I wondered how long it would take. You two were meant to be together." As Lainey and I exchanged shocked looks, Nat put his arm around Rosa, who tucked herself up against him as she greeted us, and I began to feel maybe I'd stepped into a modern version of one of Shakespeare's plays where everyone suddenly swaps partners. It was bizarre, and I was relieved to see that Amy and Scotty were still very much together.

The atmosphere was light as we walked across Pulteney Bridge and down the narrow steps, past the tables outside the pub and onto the grassy bank. Quite a few people were picnicking there, so we wandered around, found a space and sat down.

It was such a great couple of hours. We fooled around, talked (though not about anything serious), and I watched the sun catch Lainey's hair and reflect sparkles from her eyes. You know those moments when you feel that, whatever has happened and whatever is going to happen, this here and now is a perfect moment? It felt like the old days, before I got famous, when we were just mates together and I was with the girl of my dreams. Lainey seemed thrilled about Nat and Rosa, and went over to sit and chat with them for a few minutes before hugging both of them and then coming back to lie down with her head in my lap and her hand in mine.

After a while, Scotty asked me how my head was, and I realised that Amy must have told him about Galway – either that, or he'd seen it in the papers. I shrugged it off. He steered the conversation towards Lainey's hacker and the fire, and asked whether I thought Chris may have been involved. That really shook me up – it simply hadn't occurred to me. I thought carefully. "I really don't think so," I mused. "He's good with computers, but I don't think he's that good. And he drives a customised Beetle. What could his motive have been, anyway?"

"Maybe that his cousin was going out with you and he wanted to make sure Lainey stayed out of the picture?" he asked with a shrug.

By then everyone was leaning forward, listening. "The thing is," I said, "she was hardly what you'd call my girlfriend, apart from in her own head. We got on really well until she turned into a bunny boiler, but we actually only met a few times before she joined us on tour." I squeezed Lainey's hand.

Scotty leaned back. "Oh well, it was just a thought. He seems to resent you a lot."

"Dave booted him out of the band," I mumbled. "The whole thing is a mess."

Amy, who's a sensitive soul, clearly saw that I was uncomfortable and changed the subject. We all ended up getting drinks and sandwiches and sat talking for another hour or so. Then Thomas phoned and asked me to come home with Lainey. The police had some news.

CHAPTER 49

LAINEY

For a while it had felt like old times, resting against Kieran in a bubble of love, surrounded by friends who'd been there for me through so many ups and downs. The call from Thomas shocked me back to the present, and we were both quiet on our way back to the house. Kieran put his arm around me, not caring who took phone photos – and, to be honest, I didn't care either. The boy I'd loved for so long loved me, too, and that was all that mattered.

Ian and Sally, the police officers who'd visited earlier, were sitting on the sofa by the window when we entered the living room. Thomas, Jack and Aunt Bee, on the fireside sofa, looked up and smiled, and Thomas asked us to sit down. We sat.

Ian came over to us and showed us some photos. "Do you recognise this car?" he asked.

Kieran looked carefully and nodded. "Yes, it looks as if it could be the one that was behind us," he said.

They'd managed to get the number plate from one of the traffic cameras, and traced it to someone called Angela Cariss in London. Neither of us had ever heard of her. Ian didn't look surprised.

"Our local officers visited Ms. Cariss, and she insisted that she hadn't left London in weeks. Her alibi bore out under scrutiny, so we know it wasn't her. However …." He paused, and Kieran and I instinctively leaned forward. "When we checked the car, we found evidence of a petrol spill in the boot, so we questioned her further. She didn't want to say any more, but after being reminded of the seriousness of the situation, she admitted that she'd loaned her car to a friend regularly, including the day before, and had only got it back this morning."

By now my heart was beating uncomfortably fast. Kieran and I exchanged glances. Ian took the photos back and handed them to Sally before sitting down again.

"Is the name Saffron Wells familiar to you?" Sally asked. Kieran gasped.

"Oh God," he groaned. "Was it Saffie?"

Sally nodded. "She's now in custody. A search led us to discover a pair of jeans in the washing machine with petrol on them. Fortunately the machine hadn't been turned on, so the evidence is intact."

"Are you sure it was her? I mean, there could be another explanation for the petrol," Kieran stuttered. He looked utterly stunned.

Sally explained that she'd confessed, and that they'd also taken her laptop and found evidence that she'd been involved in a number of hacking incidents, including tampering with my emails and Facebook account. She'd also confessed to using her friend's car to drive to Bath and follow me. So, I really had been watched.

Poor Kieran. He looked utterly devastated, and blamed himself for all the stress I'd been through and for putting our lives at risk. Ian looked hard at him. I wouldn't want to be on the wrong side of the law and having to deal with him, that was for sure!

"This is not your fault," he stated baldly. "Her parents are in Australia, but we spoke to them and the reason she came back to England was because she has a history of stalking and minor misdemeanours, and they sent her over to try and give her a fresh start. Unfortunately, she'd been obsessed by you for some time, and getting to you was easy, given that her cousin is in your band."

"Was ...." Kieran interjected quickly. Ian nodded.

"Ah, well if he's no longer ... er ... involved with you, that can only be a positive move," he asserted.

Kieran looked utterly lambasted (Mum's WOD a couple of weeks ago).

Ian continued. "Apparently Miss Wells had followed your

previous relationship with Lainey with unusual interest." He looked directly at me and I squirmed. "She suspected that you may get back together, and was determined to ensure that wouldn't happen."

Kieran's golden skin turned a sickly shade. "Oh God," he whispered. I took one of his hands in both of mine. Ian and Sally stood up.

"We'll be in touch," Ian said. "There will be a court case, and you'll be needed as witnesses. But," and he smiled suddenly. It transformed his face. "I don't think you need to worry now she's been caught. You can relax and get on with your lives."

They left amid a chorus of thanks, and then Thomas made a huge pot of tea and insisted we all add sugar to it to help with the shock. We sat quietly. Really, what could we say?

I felt so sad for Kieran that he'd been manipulated. It was clear he blamed himself for everything that had happened. Aunt Bee and Jack insisted on cooking dinner, and Thomas insisted equally strongly on co-cooking, so Kieran and I went up to his room, with Molly at our heels. It should have felt good to know. We should have been relieved. Instead, there was a heaviness in the air that even the laughter from the kitchen couldn't seem to dispel.

CHAPTER 50

KIERAN

We sat on the edge of my bed, and I looked sideways at Lainey, feeling unbearable guilt. She looked back at me, and she knew. Slowly she pushed me down onto the duvet and lay beside me, propped up on her elbows so that she could look into my eyes. I gazed at the green glints in hers, thinking how much I loved her and how easily I could have lost her forever.

It was as if she could read my mind, and she kept telling me that it was okay, that everything would be fine now. She traced the outline of my face with a finger, and stroked it across my lip until I had no other choice but to smile. Then she leaned over and brushed her lips against mine.

"I love you, Kieran Kamau," she whispered. "We're together, and that's all that matters. No-one was hurt. We're all safe. And we have a bright, sparkly future ahead."

There are moments in life when you know that, whatever happens, everything will be fine. I felt Lainey's warm breath on my cheek and it was like a magical breeze that blew away all my doubts and fears. Not that I doubted her, but hearing Ian and Sally talk about Saffie had made me very afraid for her. Somehow I knew now that whatever the future held for both of us, we'd face it together.

I pulled Lainey down so that we were lying on our sides, facing each other. When our lips met it felt like nothing else in the world existed.

Later, after we'd been called down for dinner, and helped clear up afterwards, we went back to my room. "I want to play you a song from the new album," I told her, and I played "World of Sighs," the song of love, loss and yearning that I'd written during my lowest ebb.

Afterwards I kissed the tears from her eyes. "That was how it felt to be without you," I said.

CHAPTER 51

LAINEY

Love is only one of the steps on the path to growing up - but it's an important one. First love cuts deep, it opens us up in ways we could never have imagined. I loved Kieran from the very first moment we met over broken eggs on a hot pavement and squashed tomatoes rolling all over the road. I'd cared deeply about Nat, but it wasn't the same, and I know now that nothing ever can be. What we have is something that can't be replicated with anyone else.

Mum would (and does) say that we're soulmates and are meant to be together. She reminded me recently about the tarot reading she'd done for me, and how the outcome card was the Two of Cups, Love, and the influence of that card on my future was the Four of Wands, a sense of completeness, of coming home. And this time I agreed that she was right.

We've both changed, Kieran and me. He's accepted his gifts and the fact that the world wants pieces of him because of those. And he doesn't look at anyone but me with that amazing tenderness that he lets his music describe. I think part of his magic is that his music brings out those feelings in those who listen to it. After all, everyone wants to love and be loved.

Kieran loves me and I love him. I'm stronger than I used to be; more confident. I don't care what photos of us appear in the papers, and I don't worry about BHDs or who could be lurking around a corner with a camera. I paint a lot, developing my skills with a sense of excitement and anticipation about what I'll learn when I start college. Some (well, lots) are portraits of Kieran, and it's as if each brushstroke is a way of bringing him even closer. He loves those paintings.

Yesterday we went with Thomas to the Bath Natural Burial Meadow, to visit the tree that marked Estelle's final resting place. It was incredibly peaceful there, and we sat beside the tree and looked at the delicate wild flowers dipping their heads in the breeze. Thomas took sprigs of rosemary, for remembrance, and we all laid them gently against the tree trunk and talked about what a special person Estelle was, and how much she meant to us. I think she would have liked that.

We don't talk much about Saffie or the upcoming court case – not because it worries us, but because it feels like it's already in the past. We'd rather focus on now and our future together. Soon Kieran will be going back into the studio with Freddie, Mike and Jamal, their new drummer, and then he'll start filming with Jack, so while he's home we make the most of every moment. We see Amy and Scotty often, and sometimes Rosie and Nat join us, too. There's no awkwardness, just friendship, and that feels like such a precious gift.

In just a few days Aunt Bee and Jack will be married. Jack already feels like family, and so does Thomas. I look at the people in my life, even Mum and Dom, who just get more and more weird in a harmless sort of way (Mum insisted on cleansing my room with sweetgrass and sage when I went back home) and I think how incredibly lucky I am.

The End

www.ingramcontent.com/pod-product-compliance
Lightning Source LLC
Chambersburg PA
CBHW060425260626
47161CB00005B/1781